Gross

**She didn't resist when Captain Gringo kissed
her and began exploring her body . . .**

And everything he touched and tasted was as
soft and as sweet as angel food cake. Suddenly,
though, she purred, "My comrades in the mountains
have no machine guns at all. You must help us to
get them so we can fight Presidente Diaz."

"We'll talk about it later," he said with a smile.

She smiled back coyly, but then she stripped as
fast as she could. He pulled her close.

Later, as she pulsated she proclaimed, "If
you're half as good with a machine gun, El Presidente Diaz is doomed!"

Novels by Ramsay Thorne

Published by
WARNER BOOKS

Renegade #17

SLAUGHTER IN SINALOA

by
Ramsay Thorne

WARNER BOOKS

A Warner Communications Company

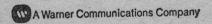

Renegade #17

SLAUGHTER
IN
SINALOA

Captain Gringo wasn't looking for a woman or any other kind of trouble as he sat alone at a sidewalk cantina table facing the main plaza of San José. The sun was setting, so the evening paseo would be starting soon. Captain Gringo didn't intend to take part in it. The paseo was a neat way to pick up *muchachas*. But he had a *muchacha,* one who'd be getting off work in about an hour. He'd been keeping company with her since getting back to the comparative safety of San José, and he saw no need to look for another. The girls of Costa Rica were renowned for their good looks and relatively sweet dispositions. Old Maria lived up to the rep and then some. So why change horses in midstream?

Captain Gringo didn't intend to. It made him appreciate his pleasantly passionate Maria even more, to sit here sipping cerveza in smug anticipation as the purple shadows lengthened, the trade winds promised a cool long night of loving, and the losers started prowling out there in the plaza.

The paseo wasn't a bad way to meet a broad, if a guy liked to walk a lot. The way the game was played down here in the tropics was perhaps more civilized, or at least less complicated, than the way a guy got laid back in the States. After supper, all the single lads and lassies told the old folks they were going for a stroll to settle their tummies. Then, everyone who wasn't married, going steady, or deformed, headed for the plaza. The guys circled the plaza one way. The gals strolled against the male current. Since it was understood that proper young ladies wouldn't *think* of speaking to or even smiling at a gentleman they'd never been introduced to, their usual chaperons stayed home by tacit agreement. The results were predictable, albeit sometimes exhausting. A guy was almost supposed to bump into an oncoming señorita at least three times as each circled the whole damned square before he got around to nodding at her in passing. She, of course, paid no attention to him until he'd nodded politely a half-dozen times or so and given her a chance to check out all the other good-looking guys at the paseo that evening. If she decided on anyone, she had the option of nodding back, or, if she was really hot, smiling.

The civilized part was that nobody ever had to feel rejected. If an ugly girl wasn't nodded to by a boy she fancied, she could always tell herself he was too shy to make advances. It worked as well for ugly boys. No gal ever told him she thought he was a miserable toad. She just went on ignoring him until he decided she was too shy, too. The paseo lasted until everyone had met somebody or gotten too tired walking to give a damn. Captain Gringo watched with an indulgent smile as the fun and games began. The early arrivals, as usual, were the very young and/or very desperate. There was nothing in a skirt out there a grown man would want to mess with.

So he kept an eye on the guys until he had them all checked out as harmless locals he'd seen before. He and his sidekick, Gaston, were as safe here in San José as two wanted outlaws could be in any part of Latin America. But that was no reason to start being careless. Costa Rica had a relatively stable government and no extradition treaty with any of the countries where Captain Gringo and Gaston Verrier were wanted. But when a knock-around guy has a dead-or-alive price on his head, he can't afford bad habits. Letting down one's guard was a bad habit that a Yank wanted for desertion, murder, and fighting on the losing side more than once could ill afford!

Getting drunk was another. So, he nursed his schooner of cerveza and lit a Havana claro while he watched the paseo and waited for Maria. Old Gaston, too, had said he might drop by the plaza that evening. The two soldiers of fortune hadn't spent as much time together as usual since coming back to San José. The whole point of this informal furlough in one of the few banana republics that saw no need of their services had been to see a little less of each other. Gaston was about the only guy down here whom Captain Gringo could trust, up to a point, but they'd been getting on each other's nerves, as well as watching each other's back, of late in the field. Aside from being pretty fair fighting men, the two soldiers of fortune had little in common. Gaston Verrier was old enough to be the tall American's father. Captain Gringo was a West Point-trained ex-officer of the U.S. Army. Old Gaston had deserted the French Legion as a gunnery sergeant. The only things they really agreed on was that it probably felt bad to get killed and it definitely felt better to sleep with almost any woman than with each other.

But, though each had gone his own way since escaping back to Costa Rica after that last wild job up north, their funds and hence their vacation time were beginning to run low. Gaston had said he knew a guy who knew another guy who might have a job for them. Captain Gringo hoped Maria would show up first. They weren't *that* broke, and Maria hadn't started to nag him yet.

He knew she would in another week or so. Dames were like that. It just couldn't be helped. Men and women both deserved something better than each other. But there wasn't anything else he wanted to try, so what the hell. Meanwhile, he and old Maria were still in the honeymoon stage of their relationship. So, she probably wouldn't start nagging him to marry her and get a decent job for . . . oh, maybe another week or so. He'd been sleeping with her for three, had enough cash to last a full month, and that was why they called it a honeymoon, right?

A willowy brunette with an organdy rose pinned to the hip of her red fandango skirt smiled down at Captain Gringo as she passed his table. He didn't smile back. He had to think about that, and he knew she'd be back as she completed her circuit of the plaza.

He blew a thoughtful smoke ring after her and watched her hips sway as the smoke made a bull's-eye of her ass. She swayed good, and her face wasn't bad, either. He wondered, idly, why she'd flirted with him so soon. Captain Gringo didn't suffer false modesty. His mirror and more than one woman had assured him he wasn't a bad-looking guy when he'd had a shave and wasn't mad at anybody. The *muchacha* in the red skirt was of course Hispanic, and he supposed his blond hair and Anglo features were a novelty to her. From the bold way she walked, he figured she knew all the local talent worth knowing, in a biblical sense. She could be a *puta*. It was an unwritten rule of the paseo that neither whores nor married women were supposed to pick guys up like that in the plaza. But if everyone in Latin America obeyed all the rules, soldiers of fortune like himself and Gaston wouldn't get nearly as many job offers.

He decided to pass on her offer. She was as pretty as Maria and offered a very interesting change of pace, but he'd learned, the hard way, that when dames down here acted too good to be true, they generally were.

He'd nursed his beer to a stale puddle in the bottom of the schooner by now. He looked at his watch, saw he still had time to kill, and held up a finger to the waiter lounging in the doorway under the awning.

The waiter ducked inside to get him another. Meanwhile, a woman with ash-blond hair and wearing a black dress sat down uninvited across from him at the tin table. He didn't say anything. He had to think about this, too.

She was dressed like a European or North American, with a matching small black hat and veil perched atop her upswept blond hair. The veil covered her face to the tip of her nose. But she looked familiar as well as very, very pretty. As he tried to place her, she said, "I heard you were in town, Dick. I'm still very cross with you, but I need your help again."

The waiter came back with Captain Gringo's cerveza. The waiter looked surprised to see the blonde sitting there. That made two of them. The tall Yank asked the girl what she was drinking, and when she said gin and tonic, the waiter said he'd be right on it.

As soon as they were alone again, she said, "I have to run over to the west coast and pick up something in Puntarenas. It's over fifty miles, and they tell me bandits have been stopping the stagecoaches again."

He didn't answer. He knew the face. But the world was full of ash-blondes, and somehow everything didn't fit together right in his memory. She asked, "Is your friend Gaston still working with you, Dick?"

He said, "Maybe. I hadn't heard about banditos on the Puntarenas Trail. Costa Rica has a pretty good national guard, and if anyone's gone into business for himself in the hills to the west, I'm sure your coach will rate an

11

armed escort. I'm an ordnance officer, not a professional bodyguard. I doubt you'd want to pay my going rates, even if you could afford 'em."

The waiter came back out and put her drink in front of her before she said, a bit coldly, "I already paid you, Dick. I gave you a thousand dollars in Cayenne that time, and you never showed up as we'd agreed, remember?"

He remembered that time, and the dame who had almost gotten him killed. He studied her new hair and dress as he let blue smoke trickle out his nostrils. Then he nodded and said, "You used to be a brunette with a phony French accent. They told us later that you were a German agent working to stir up more trouble for the French over the Dreyfus affair. I thought you'd been arrested, Claudette."

"Pooh, and I heard you'd been eaten by crocodiles on the Hondo. Never mind who I'm working for these days, Dick. The point is that I gave you earnest money and you never showed up to do the job!"

He took a sip of cerveza and said, "We showed. Gaston and I went to the address you gave us and walked into a goddamn ambush. I didn't see *you* there when those effing bounty hunters shot it out with us. We blasted every son-ofabitch laying for us, and they were all in your house in Cayenne!"

She looked sincerely startled as she said, "But Dick, there was no gunfight at the address I gave you! Why would we have . . . Wait, I remember. There *was* a gunfight that night in Cayenne! It happened about two blocks away from where we were to meet. But not at the address I gave you. I swear it!"

He nodded and said, "Gaston and me figured it out later. A Yankee bounty hunter called Klondike set us up by marking phony house numbers with chalk. That still means somebody in that phony-baloney rescue operation of yours was in on it. Klondike never had time to give me all the details when I turned the tables on him. He died sort of sudden."

She wrinkled her pert nose and said, "I can't tell you if one of the other agents working with me played us false or not. It is true most of them were picked up by the French constabulary, thanks to a tip from you and British Intelligence, you mean old thing. As you see, I got away. What are we going to do about that thousand-dollar advance, Dick?"

It was a good question. Captain Gringo had about eight hundred in cash at the moment and needed it all. He sipped some cerveza as she said, "I paid you to help me and you never delivered. Now I need help again. It's only fifty miles or so, Dick."

He didn't answer. She said, "They say it's an overnight trip by stage. You can be back here by this weekend, and as for a few bandits . . ."

"Screw the bandits." He growled, adding, "It's you I'm worried about. Tell me more about this job of yours. Are you still working for *Der Kaiser,* Claudette?"

"Of course not. Like yourself, I work for the highest bidder, and we both know the Brits broke up that operation in Cayenne. I'm working for a private syndicate now. French, if you have to know their nominal nationality. You know, of course, about the stalled Panama Canal situation?"

"Yeah. One of the reasons it's stalled was because of Gaston and me helping out some Panamanian rebels a while back. I'm not about to go to Panama City with you, Claudette. The Colombian authorities down there don't like me, and they've got a Colonel Maldonado working for them who's almost as good as me!"

"Pooh, I said I only wanted to dash over to the Costa Rican seaport of Puntarenas. We'll be coming right back."

"We? You mean it's a round trip? You must want to

be guarded pretty good, Claudette. Which way are you headed and to deliver what?"

She hesitated, then said, "If you must know, I am to meet a coastal schooner in Puntarenas. They're going to give me something. I am to see it gets back here to the capital. That's all there is to the mission." '

He took out his watch to check the time. She said, "You owe me *money*, darling."

That was true. He knew she'd called him darling to remind him of other things she might think he still owed her, damn it. He felt a tingle in his pants and tried to ignore it. The pale cool Claudette was built nothing at all like his short dusky Maria, and he couldn't help wondering if Claudette had bleached her hair all over.

On the other hand, the adventuress across the table was about as safe to handle as an open bucket of bushmasters, and, while her story made some sense, he couldn't help remembering the last time he'd made a date with her. He'd walked into a machine-gun ambush at close quarters!

She reached a hand across the table and placed it on the back of his as she slid a high-button shoe tip against his mosquito boot under the table and said, softly, "I don't have anyone else to turn to, Dick. I don't have enough money to hire any local bravos. I don't get paid until I deliver. But if you get me and a certain package back from Puntarenas safe and sound, I may be able to swing a bonus for you and Gaston."

As if he'd heard his name being paged, Gaston Verrier materialized out of nowhere and sat down between them, saying, "You are looking lovely this evening, m'mselle. One must assume the French constabulary failed in their duties again?"

Claudette smiled wanly and said, "Good-evening, M'sieur Verrier. I am flattered you remembered me at once. I fear Dick, here, may have trouble remembering old, ah, friends."

Gaston shrugged and said, "He is younger and better-looking than I. So naturally he has more, ah, friends to remember."

Then Gaston turned to Captain Gringo and said, "Speaking of friends, Dick, I just came from the *bodega* where your Maria is employed. They are taking inventory this evening and she asked me to tell you she may be very late, *hein?*"

Claudette sniffed and said, "Maria, eh? I might have known. But about that thousand dollars, Dick . . ."

Captain Gringo shushed her with a wave of his cigar as he turned to Gaston and asked, "Could we scrape up a thousand to spare between us, Gaston?"

Gaston shook his head and said, *"Mes non,* all the banks are closed for the night, my old and impossibly generous. I thought we had settled the matter of that droll cash advance in Cayenne, *hein?*"

Gaston turned to Claudette and said, "You hired us to meet you at a certain place with a view to doing something about the *très fatigue affaire* Dreyfus. *Eh bien,* we went to the address you gave us and nearly got shot. And later, when we were dragged into the business about Captain Dreyfus despite ourselves and tried to rescue him from Devil's Island, he said he did not wish to be rescued since he had friends in Paris working on a full pardon for him at the moment. Add it all up, m'mselle, and you can see we owe you nothing for the modest front money you offered us, *non?*"

"Offered like hell! I *gave* you two scamps a thousand dollars, U.S.!"

"Now, now, let us not get picky, m'mselle. The point is that whether we did exactly as you asked or not, we don't *have* the money anymore. So why are we having this tedious discussion, *hein?*"

She repeated to Gaston her plans about running over to the west coast and back. Captain Gringo kicked him under the table, but Gaston still asked Claudette what she was supposed to pick up and deliver.

She looked down hesitantly, sighed, and said, "Oh, very well. If you must know, it's emeralds. Colombia has this ridiculous export duty on gemstones the damned old Andes are absolutely filled with, and . . ."

"I see the light," Gaston cut in, adding, "Your friends cannot take emeralds out via the usual railroad across Panama province because of the *fatigué* customs officials in both Panama City and Colón. On the other hand, Costa Rica takes a more casual attitude than the Colombian junta and tends not to notice visitors who don't happen to be biting anyone on the shin at the moment. That, of course, is why Dick and I lay up here between jobs, and why you and your syndicate find it such a friendly country to do business in, *hein?*"

She said, "Exactly. As I just told Dick, here, there is no danger involved in meeting the schooner and picking up the rough emeralds. I was planning to make the run alone, until I heard there were bandits in the hills to the west."

Gaston smiled noncommittally as he stared at Captain Gringo. The tall American said nothing. Claudette said, "I'll forget the thousand and pay you each a hundred a day after we get back. I don't have a machine gun for you, but I have a brace of .44-40 Winchesters if you need them."

"We'd need them," sighed Captain Gringo, adding, "if we were going with you. There's no way you'd smuggle anything through happy-go-lucky Costa Rican lawmen after arriving by stage with a machine gun braced out a window." Then he turned to Gaston and said, "You know all the roughnecks in these parts, Gaston. Couldn't you scout up a couple of tough hairpins who'd work for a hundred a day?"

16

Mais oui! I could hire a *platoon* of rogues for that kind of money. The complication would be hiring *honest* rogues though. M'mselle would no doubt be safe enough going west, empty-handed. Coming back with a bag of untraceable emeralds in the rough might be another matter!"

Claudette nodded and said, "You two are the only rogues I can trust. You have to help me, Dick. My hotel's not far. Why don't we talk about it some more as I show you the new weapons I just bought?"

Captain Gringo hesitated. He had a pretty good idea what she wanted to show him. But even if she *did* trust him, he didn't return her trust worth a damn. Gaston stood up and said, "Guard our seats and we'll be right back, m'mselle. Come, Dick, I think I'd better have a fatherly talk with you, *hein?*"

The blonde remained seated at the table as the two soldiers of fortune moved out of earshot, under an archway. Gaston said, "I vote *oui,* Dick. What have we to lose? The last time we worked with her we made an easy thousand, *non?*"

"It wasn't that easy. We damn near got killed. Do you buy her story this time, Gaston? The last time she tried to hire us, she handed us a real line of bullshit."

"True. She may be shitting us now. But what of it? We could use the extra cash, and it makes me uneasy to have a woman wandering about San José weeping that we owe her a thousand dollars."

"Yeah. The cops here don't bother us because they see no reason to. But there could be limits, even to a Costa Rican lawman's tolerance, if she bitched to them about us. But do you think she could? She's not exactly as pure as the driven snow, either."

Gaston shrugged and said, "Why worry about the unpredictable moods of a woman when it seems so easy to

17

keep her happy, *hein?* There are no bandits in the mountains to the west. None I have heard of, at any rate. The ride to the coast by stage will be fast and reasonably comfortable. Why not go along with her droll tale and discharge our modest obligations to the attractive pest, *hein?* Who knows, we may even find out what she is really up to."

Captain Gringo smiled crookedly and said, "You don't buy that story about smuggled emeralds either, eh?"

"*Mais non.* It is all too complicated. Why go to the trouble of sneaking illegal gemstones through even a nice banana republic when they have a clean run north to the gem market of San Francisco, *hein?*"

"Maybe they want to smuggle 'em back to France?"

"I doubt that very much. Nobody pays more for jewelry than your Yankee nabobs by the Golden Gate. Europe is not only *très* lousy with gems, legal and otherwise, but three times as far by sea as *jolie* Frisco. I hazard a guess she is still working for young Kaiser Willy. The German navy is doubtless still interested in how things are going at the Pacific end of the bogged-down Panama Canal project and . . ."

"Gotcha. The old shell game again. She'll probably really pick up some rough emeralds, or something that looks like rough emeralds, and ask us to guard the hell out of 'em while she packs stolen or copied documents in the lining of another carpetbag."

"*Oui.* Leave that part to me, Dick. You watch her emeralds and, if possible, distract her with *amour* long enough for me to steal or make a copy of our own, depending on opportunity."

Captain Gringo looked blank and asked, "What the hell for? We don't work for Colombia. What the hell do we care if the Germans are spying on them or not? The Kaiser seems to be a nasty little prick. But the junta running things to the south is no better."

"*Eh bien*. And meanwhile nobody can figure out when and if the triple-titted canal will be built, or by whom. *Der Kaiser* won't be the only prick willing to pay good money for whatever Claudette and her chums have to deliver to the German embassy here in San José, *hein?*"

"Jesus, you're right! *That*'s why she only wants to deliver her so-called smuggled goods here to the capital, smack in the middle of the highlands!"

"*Qui*. If the intent was to smuggle them to France, she would have wanted us to accompany her all the way down to Limón, on the east coast. There *are* a few bandits haunting the lowland jungles down that way. This whole droll scheme is a snipe hunt, as you Yanks say. But, as you also say, what the hell, it's a pretty snipe, with possible added attractions in the form of ill-gotten gains to sell to the highest bidder along Embassy Row when we get back, *hein?*"

Captain Gringo nodded and said, "It's starting to make sense. Sort of. There's still a piece missing. Why is she hiring us at all if she isn't picking up real emeralds and there aren't any bandits along the trail?"

Gaston shrugged and said, "Perhaps she thinks there may be, *non?* On the other hand, since we know she is a spy, and others may know she is a spy, she may have some other spies after her, *non?*"

"That makes even more sense. But whose spies? The States's, Great Britain's, France's? Hell, for all we know, the Imperial Russian Navy may be just as interested as Germany in the Panama Canal project. How do we find out? I doubt like hell Claudette's about to tell us!"

Gaston shrugged and replied, "What does it matter, Dick? We are soldiers of fortune. We fight for the flag of the highest bidder. Up to now, nobody but Claudette has offered us a centavo. You run along and see her guns and other charms. I shall stay here and make your apologies to Maria when and if she arrives, *hein?* Don't look

19

at me like that, Dick. Of course I won't try to steal your girl while you set things up with Claudette in order to rob her blind!"

The little hotel Claudette led him to surprised Captain Gringo. He never would have picked it as a hideout. Prices in the tropics were so low that while it might have passed as second-rate in the States, down here it was the sort of dump the local cops tended to keep an eye on, with good reason. He wondered idly whether she was broke or just had a lot to learn about traveling submerged.

There were some advantages to the shabby little hotel near the plaza. A wan, wee lamp was burning in the vestibule, but there was no desk clerk or any other sign that the landlord gave a damn who came or went. The well-dressed blonde led him up a narrow flight of rickety stairs and along a dark narrow hallway to her corner room. She struck a match as they entered. Joints like this one had never heard of Thomas Alva Edison and couldn't have afforded the new Edison bulbs if they had.

Claudette lit a candle on the washstand near the door and moved over to the shuttered windows to open the jalousies. She said, "I hid the guns under the mattress. Let's hope they're still there."

They were. Captain Gringo lifted a corner of the mattress and slid out the two Winchesters. The carbines were spanking new and, when he levered open the chambers, loaded. He nodded and leaned both guns in a corner by the bed, as the blonde took a pasteboard carton from under the pillows and asked, "Are you still carrying that same .38, Dick?"

He smiled crookedly and said, "Hardly the same one. But, given my druthers, I favor a double-action .38 under the same old armpit. Why?"

She held out the carton and said, "Extra ammunition for your sidearms, if you and Gaston should need it."

He stuffed the carton in the side pocket of his linen jacket and said, "You must really expect a lot of trouble between here and the coast, doll."

Then he took off his sombrero and jacket and sat down on the bed to take off his boots. Claudette blinked and asked, "Just what do you think you're doing, Dick?"

He said, "Make sure the door's locked. What the hell do you think I'm doing? Enough of this foreplay. Take off your clothes."

She moved to lock the barrel bolt between them and the hall, but said, "You certainly seem to take a lot for granted, Dick! I know we, ah, used to know each other well. But I'm still a little cross with you, and . . ."

"Look, do you want to be friends again or don't you?" he cut in, adding, "You were the one who asked me up here, doll face. I just stood up a nice little enchilada for you. But it's not too late to keep my date with her, if you've suddenly vowed celibacy for some dumb reason."

"You're a beast." She sighed, unpinning her hat and hanging it up as she snuffed out the candle. There was enough light through the open windows to follow the rest of her motions as Claudette undressed, muttering to herself that all men were alike.

He beat her into bed, not having as much to remove and having started earlier. Claudette got down to her corset, knickers, and long black stockings before she suddenly giggled and asked him, "Will you be staying the night, dear?"

He said, "I'd better not. Have to check with Gaston later at our own hotel. Why?"

"I'd better leave this corset on, then. I have a few last-minute errands, too, and it takes forever to get in and out of the silly thing."

She moved over to the bed and slid off her black silk

knickers. He saw that, sure enough, she was still really a brunette. As she got into bed with him, he took her in his arms, rolled atop her, and said, "Hi. Long time no see."

She started to protest his matter-of-fact approach. But he kissed her to shut her up as he spread her silk-sheathed thighs and parted her pubic hair with his erection. She gasped but tongued him as he drove it into her to the roots and started pounding. He wasn't usually this brutal with a woman. But the nice thing about looking up old bedmates was that you knew right off how they liked it best. This wasn't the first time he'd been in Claudette. The last time; she'd practically raped *him!*

He raised himself on braced elbows to let them both breathe as the action heated up and the damned cinch around her narrow waist began to chafe his own bare belly. The view was inspiring. Claudette had an hourglass figure even when she wasn't trying to cut it in twain with a black band of whalebone and silk lace. In the romantic glow of the streetlamp through the nearby window, her bobbing breasts were highlighted in old gold and shaded into deep purple. Her face wasn't bad, either, as she smiled up at him and said, "I'd forgotten how good it was with you, darling. Have you been true to me since last we met like this in Cayenne?"

He laughed down at her and replied, "About as true to you as you've been to me, I'd say. I like that new trick you picked up with those internal muscles, doll. But could you move your ass a bit more?"

"Oh, you're just horrid!" she protested, raising her knees to hug his hips with her thighs as she started bouncing better but still went on milking him with her educated vaginal contractions. They both went crazy for a while, came together, as old pals tended to, then lay still in each other's arms as they recovered their wind and lowered their guards a bit.

He was soaking silently in her when Claudette broke the contented calm by chuckling fondly and murmuring, "I'm glad you haven't changed ,Dick. I confess I've always been a little coy, for a dedicated sex maniac."

"Yeah, I noticed you seemed a little prim at first this evening. How come? You must have known I'd lay you as soon as we were alone, doll."

"I was hoping you'd still want to. But this means a change in plans. I was hoping to go right back to the plaza with you as soon as we picked up the guns and ammo. But the damage is done, and now it's too late to catch the night stage to the coast. So would you like to try some dog-style?"

That sounded reasonable. He dismounted and let her roll over on her knees and elbows across the bed before putting it back in her, standing barefoot on the floor as he grasped one of her hip bones in each hand and proceeded to pleasure her in a less romantic but deeper way as she arched her spine to take it all.

Another advantage of dog-style, with old friends, was that it was easier to chat in this position. So as he screwed her, he asked her, conversationally, why the hell she wanted to travel at night by coach, adding, "Guys who stop coaches for a living *prefer* moonlight and deserted roads, doll. It's a hell of a lot safer traveling by day."

"Is it? Oooh, that's too deep! Could you . . . ah, yes, that's better. I thought the night coach was better because it arrives in Puntarenas about nine in the morning, while it's still cool. It's hotter than blazes in the lowlands at this time of the year, and we may have to wait on the docks awhile."

He caught movement out of the corner of his eye and glanced that way, and saw they were reflected in the mirror on the far wall. It was amazing that anything that felt so good could look so vulgar. It inspired him to move his bare ass faster as he asked her, "How come we have

23

to hang around on the docks, doll? I thought we were *meeting* a schooner."

"We are. But for security reasons nobody told me its name. My contact with the emeralds knows me on sight. He'll be disguised, of course. I'm to wait at a certain sidewalk cantina along the waterfront. That's another reason I need a male escort and . . . Oooh, you *are* male, aren't you?"

She started moving her lamplit rump to meet his thrusts by flexing her spine, and now, although he was hitting bottom with every stroke, she didn't seem to mind it at all. It looked wild as hell in the mirror over there. Suddenly she bit down hard and pulled him after her by the dong as she fell limply across the bed. He could tell by her pulsations that she was enjoying a long protracted orgasm as he lay atop, and in, her. He withdrew, rolled her over on her back, and hooked an elbow under each of her knees to open her wide and finish it right for her. She rolled her blond head from side to side, moaning that he was killing her, as she bumped and ground her pubic bone against his. His feet were braced against the floor and his questing shaft was kissing her throbbing wet uterus when he exploded inside her again. She moaned, "Oh, me too! I can't stop coming!"

But they finally did, of course. That was the trouble with the good things in life. People could work twelve hours at a stretch in a factory, but the pleasures of food and fornication were all too fleeting. She said he was getting heavy. So he rolled off to let her fight for her second wind as he fumbled for a smoke, if he could remember where he'd dropped his damned shirt. He had to sit up to get at it. Claudette sighed up at him and said, "God, you have a lovely body, Dick. How soon do you have to leave?"

"Not right now. Just looking for my fucking cigars and a match. But let me get it straight about our pickup on the coast. Do you have a particular time as well as place to meet this mysterious sailor, honey?"

"No, dear. They can see the cantina tables from aboard the schooner. But about the night coach and our time of arrival . . ."

"Yeah, sitting at a tin table under an afternoon sun in this neck of the woods isn't just asking for heat stroke. It could make even a Costa Rican cop curious as hell. But look, if we catch the morning coach it'll get us to Puntarenas around three in the afternoon. *La siesta* lasts till four or later in the dry season. So, while it'll be hot enough to fry an egg on the pavement as we arrive, not a damned soul will spot us arriving. We can beeline from the coach station to a shady posada I know there, tear off a bath and some more of this to recover from the long dusty trip, and meet your smuggling buddies in the cool of evening when nobody will notice us as we stroll the waterfront, right?"

She thought and said, "That makes sense. I'm glad I looked you up again, Dick. I confess I have a lot to learn about the kind of life I'm forced to lead."

"Don't tell me how a nice girl like you got into this business, *por favor*. The last time you told me the story of your life it was all bullshit, remember?"

She laughed and said, "A girl has to have some kind of cover story, dear. But you're right. Ships that pass in the night don't have to send false signals."

"As long as their gunports are closed," he amended, placing his unlit claro on the bed table and adding, "Can't find a match. But the hell with it. A guy can *smoke* any old time."

He lay back down beside her and took her in his arms once more. She kissed him, tongued him, and ran her hand down to fondle his semierection. She murmured, "Oh, the poor thing seems to be tired. Mama had better kiss it and make it well."

That sounded friendly. So he rolled on his back and relaxed as she started kissing her way down his belly. He tried to remember if she'd done this the last time. A lot of broads had passed under the bridge since he'd first met old Claudette, and . . . and then her moist lips engulfed his flaccid flesh and he knew for sure they'd been interrupted in Cayenne before they'd gotten around to everything. He'd have never forgotten anyone who gave such nice face. Only one woman in ten really knew how to give French lessons right. Claudette was the tenth. She pursed her lips over her teeth to form a soft fleshy doughnut around his shaft as she inhaled it until her pert nose was tickling his balls with Eskimo kisses and his foreskin was getting stripped back and forth by the base of her tongue. He had no idea why she didn't gag with his growing erection so deep in her throat. But if it didn't bother *her,* it surely didn't cause *him* any discomfort!

She knew the effect she was having on his organ grinder as she sucked it even deeper. That seemed to make her even hotter, and she made little growling noises that tingled the hell out of the exposed head in her throat. He started moving his hips as he saw she could literally take fucking that way, too. She responded by cocking one leg over his chest to settle her bare groin over his own face, expectantly.

The lamplight from outside was shining on her bare buttocks and smooth naked upper thighs, and her slit glistened wetly through her dark pubic hair. He had to think about that. Captain Gringo considered himself a good sport. But while it seemed common courtesy to return such lovely favors, Claudette wasn't exactly a blushing virgin, and the trouble with a gal who screwed literally at the drop of a hat was that one suspected they screwed a lot. If he could have her easy, God only knew whom she'd submit to after a little effort!

He knew he had to do something. Claudette was

26

whimpering with desire as she bobbed her head in time with his thrusts at the other end. He licked his lips as he parted her hairy lips with his fingers. But, hell, he'd come twice in there himself, and he doubted like hell she'd been true to him since the last time he'd flung her across a bed.

He started massaging her turgid clit with two fingers as he groped with his free hand for the bed table. His questing fingers touched the unlit cigar. But that was silly. Claros were not particularly big cigars. He felt the edge of a cut glass bowl, and, yeah, as he'd remembered, there was some fruit in the bowl. He'd thought she'd left it there to nibble in bed. But as he hefted what he'd thought to be a banana, he realized it was wax.

He grinned. That was even better. Claudette gasped and almost spit out his shaft as she felt the artificial substitute entering her from the other end. Then, as he kept massaging her clit with one hand while sliding the fat wax banana in and out of her with the other, she gave a contented little sigh and tried to swallow him balls and all.

She came ahead of him, even though he'd had a head start. As he drove the wax banana in and out of her, feeling the pulsations of her excited vagina with his fingers as he worked, he knew he was almost there, too. He groaned, "Enough! I don't want to waste it even if you want to taste it!"

She giggled as he rolled her over on her own back and hurriedly swapped ends. He was afraid he was going to come in midair. So he thrust hard as he remounted her, and, although it seemed a little tight, he got it in before he could come outside her. But as he exploded inside her, Claudette gasped, "You maniac! It's the wrong hole!"

He moved experimentally, enjoying the way her rectal muscles rippled, too, as he said, "So it is. Sorry about that. Did I hurt you?"

"You know you didn't. Now don't take it out. I want to try an experiment."

Her anal opening was tight enough to keep him hard inside her that way. So he moved teasingly and said, "I'm game for this way if you are."

She was. She said, "It feels so huge back there. But put that banana in my *other* place, dear! It's starting to feel abandoned and . . ."

He laughed, found the wax banana, and rolled half off her to make room as he inserted it where she wanted it, asking, "How's that?"

She said, "Heavenly. I'd heard about a famous opera singer who made love to two men at once this way. I've always wondered what it would feel like."

He was getting hot again. He found that by rolling back atop her, with the end of the wax banana against his lower gut, he could move both real and artificial stuffing in and out of both her entrances. It seemed to drive her nuts. He liked it, too. Her internal contraction kept trying to eject both him and the banana as he worked against them with his thrusting pelvis. She gasped, "Oh, my God! I'm being fucked all over! I've never felt so filled with cock!"

That was only half true for her, while he was only in one of her openings after all. But he was grateful to whoever had thought to cheer up the drab room with artificial fruit. When he came again in her tight, throbbing rear, she came so hard that she shot the wax banana out like a watermelon seed, then pleaded, "Put it in me *right!* I'm still coming!"

He did as she asked. But, in truth, by now it was getting past pleasure and into showing off. So when she came yet again, Captain Gringo faked it and rolled off with an exhausted sigh.

She might have been showing off too. She rose from the

bed, got a washcloth from the bowl on the stand, and returned to clean him off, saying, "We'd better save some of this for Puntarenas, darling. I have to get dressed now."

"Oh, I thought you'd given up on the night coach."

"I certainly have, you horrid thing. But I have to send a wire so they'll know not to expect us in the morning. The *telegrafo*'s not far. Do you want to come with me?"

"I've already come with you. A lot. I'd better take the guns and extra pistol rounds over to my place. Gaston will be wondering what's keeping me so long."

She laughed and said, "I doubt that very much. He walked in on us the last time, rememeber?"

"Yeah. Okay, here's the form. We'll meet in the morning at the coach station. Like I said, we ought to make Puntarenas during *la siesta*. So tell your pals to expect us around sundown and . . . Wait a minute. How are you going to wire them if you don't know what boat they'll be on?"

"Silly. The people at the waterfront cantina are go-betweens. What's the matter? Do you mean to say you still don't trust me, Dick?"

He didn't answer. He was too polite to say it but, hell, he'd have licked her pussy by now if he'd really thought he could count on her to tell him the truth about anything.

Captain Gringo naturally took a dark side street on his way home with a pair of Winchesters cradled over his left elbow. So he was mildly surprised when a shadow detached itself from a doorway and fell in step with him along the dark lane. The tall American said in Spanish, "I hope you don't think I carry lots of money, amigo. It's stupid to get hurt for small change."

The other man answered in English, "I'm Carson, from

the U.S. embassy, Walker. I know where you got those carbines. We were watching her when she bought 'em the other day."

Captain Gringo didn't answer as they walked along side by side for a while. Carson said, "You wouldn't have those guns if you hadn't agreed to work for her. I don't suppose a renegade like you gives a damn who you work for, right?"

"Damned A," said Captain Gringo, adding, "You know my name, so you know my story. The official army version, anyway. I don't suppose you care what really happened back in the States, eh?"

Carson shrugged and said, "Not really. Some say you got a bum rap. Some say you're no fucking good. Since we both know Uncle Sam can't touch you here in San José, I don't give a damn either way. Let's talk about that German agent of yours, Walker."

"Is she still a German agent? That's not the way she tells it. But what the hell, if you guys say she is, who am I to argue? Is there any point to this conversation, Carson?"

"There is. Young Kaiser Willy makes President Cleveland nervous. Just like he makes everyone else with a lick of sense nervous. We don't give two hoots in hell about scum like you signing up to fight for greaser factions down here, Walker. But, renegade or not, you're still a Yank, God damn it, and that dame you're working for is out to screw Uncle Sam!"

"Hey, don't knock it until you try it. Uncle Sam could do worse. Why the hell does the embassy care about old Claudette working for Germany? Everybody has to work for somebody. Germany's not at war with the States. Can't Kaiser Willy have spies around here if he wants 'em? God knows everyone else has."

Carson shook his head and said, "The Monroe Doctrine says different. It's agreed Great Britain, France, and the

U. S. of A. have a legitimate interest in the Panama Canal project. It's none of the Kaiser's fucking business whether said canal gets built or not. The square-heads are out to fuck things up down there."

Captain Gringo chuckled and said, "That sounds fair. Everyone else has been meddling in the revolutionary movement down that way. We all know the only way the canal will ever be completed is if the Panamanian rebels win. I was down in Colombia a while back. I noticed the Colombian junta didn't like us outsiders much. They seem to resent the way everyone tries to screw up their internal affairs. I didn't know the Germans were trying to steal the Isthmus of Panama from Colombia, though I was betting on us or the Brits."

"Look, why don't you come over to the embassy with me, Walker? My boss can explain better than I what's involved in this latest German move."

Captain Gringo snorted in disbelief and asked, "Do I really look that stupid, buddy? It's true Costa Rica has no extradition treaty with the States, but let's not get silly about it! We both know that once you guys had me inside a U.S. embassy, the U.S. Marine Guard would no doubt find some ingenious way to smuggle me out of the country. Embalmed in a large diplomatic pouch, perhaps?"

"Don't talk like an asshole, Walker! We're too far from either coast even to consider taking you, alive or otherwise. This German plot is more important to us than your petty set-to with the U.S. Army. We're with the State Department, not War or Justice. I give you my word you won't be arrested if you come with me to the embassy to hear us out."

"I can hear you just as good right here, Carson. No offense, but I'd still be a U.S. Cavalry officer instead of an outlaw on the dodge if I hadn't once taken the word of a guy I knew a lot better than I know you."

31

He kept walking, so Carson had no choice but to keep pace with Captain Gringo as he sighed and said, "God damn it. Walker, the French have a legit claim to interest in the future canal, since they started the whole idea and would have finished it by now if it hadn't been for Yellow Jack and those damned Colombians blackmailing them for more money. The Brits have a legit interest because they let the U.S. Navy use their Suez Canal, and one hand washes the other. The U.S. has an even better claim because American interests bought out the French canal company when it went broke."

"Tell me something I haven't already heard before, from both sides, in the guerrilla fighting down there. Where does the Kaiser and his neat new navy fit in?"

"They don't. The German shipyards are working around the clock to catch up with the Royal Navy, and at the rate they're going, Germany will have as big and probably more modern a navy than Great Britain by the turn of the century. By then, hopefully, the Panama Canal will be in business. When, not if, Kaiser Willy decides *Der Tag* has arrived, he'll face a Royal Navy that can take considerable shortcuts through a canal he knows he'll never be able to use in wartime. The British have crown colonies in this neck of the woods. Germany doesn't, and won't, if the U.S. has anything to say about it. And the U.S will. Not even Kaiser Willy is dumb enough to get into a war with us and the Brits at the same time."

"That sounds reasonable. So what's the problem? Germany can't build any goddamn Panama Canal, no matter what they may be up to, right?"

Carson nodded, but said, "We know what they're up to, the devious bastards! Germany will never be able to use such a canal in time of war, and they know it, so they're busting a gut making sure said canal is never built! Krupp's been selling arms, at cost, to Colombia. German agents are working on both sides in the ongoing revolution down there to see that neither side can ever hope to settle the matter."

Captain Gringo nodded as he spotted the lights of his own hotel ahead. He said, "Makes sense. If I had a navy that had to go around Cape Horn to get to my Pacific islands, I think I'd make sure all my rivals had to go around the Horn a lot too. But just what do you expect me to do about all this, Carson? I don't hold a commission in any fucking navy at the moment."

"We want you to find out just what Claudette Pardeau, nee Pfalz, is picking up for the German embassy here in San José. We know she's going somewhere to pick up something. You no doubt have a better idea than we, right?"

"She didn't say," Captain Gringo lied, adding, "It's been nice talking to you, Carson. By the way, did you say something about a pardon for me if I spied on Germany for dear old Uncle Sam?"

Carson didn't answer. Captain Gringo hadn't expected him to. His voice was bitter as he nodded and said, "That's what I thought you said. I stopped a war for the U.S. Marines in Venezuela one noisy afternoon a while back, Carson. You know what I got for fighting for my old country, free? I got shit! Those same marines I helped got orders to arrest me. So I had to run like hell."

Carson looked uncomfortable and said, "Look, I know you think you got a raw deal from the U.S. Cav' that time, but . . ."

"But me no buts," Captain Gringo cut in, adding, "I don't *think* I got a raw deal, Carson. I *know* I did! I was serving my country as best I knew how when some incompetent senior officers decided to cover their own poor soldiering by hanging it all on yours truly! You might say

33

it soured me on my country right or wrong, Carson. My country was wrong as hell and I came awfully close to hanging for it!"

"Come on, Walker. You have to admit you killed a fellow officer back in the States."

"Admit it, shit, I'm proud of it! The motherfucker was fixing to hang me in the morning and he was dumb enough to gloat about it where I could get my hands on him! What would you have done, kissed his ass and gone to the gallows as requested? Sure I killed him. I'd have killed a dozen like him if I'd had to. But that's ancient history. So let's just agree that you're a good guy and I'm a bad guy and it's been nice talking to you, but not that nice. So, adios, motherfucker."

He left Carson standing on the corner as he turned it to enter his own hotel. It was a better place than Claudette's, so there was a room clerk on duty in the lobby. The room clerk knew better than to ask what he was doing with two carbines in his hands and a very annoyed look on his face as he grumped his way across the lobby and up the stairs.

He and Gaston had booked adjoining rooms, of course. He saw light under Gaston's door, so he went in. Gaston was reclining on the bed, smoking a cigar and reading, or scanning, a magazine that must have been rather naughty. Gaston was idly jerking off with his free hand.

Captain Gringo propped the guns in a corner and growled, "Didn't your folks ever tell you little boys can go blind playing with themselves?"

Gaston stuffed his tool back in his pants with a sheepish grin as he answered, "*Oui,* but I don't need glasses yet. Your Maria is a *très* inspiring *muchacha,* Dick. But, as you just saw, she was true to you when I told her you couldn't make it, or her, tonight. How did things go with m'mselle Claudette? After you laid her, I mean."

34

Captain Gringo lit a smoke for himself and sat on a chair near the bed long enough to fill Gaston in on both Claudette's plans and the U.S. embassy's apparent objections to them.

When he'd finished, Gaston sat up and said, *"Eh bein.* We had better go with her to Puntarenas, in that case."

"Are you crazy, Gaston? I was about to suggest we double-cross her again. What's in that cigar you're smoking? I just told you the goddamn U.S. government is on to her! They're watching her hotel. That's how they spotted me coming out. They may not know where she's going, or to do what, but they're bound to tail her, and us, to the stage station in the morning. Have you forgotten she's not the only person in town Uncle Sam is interested in? You and me are both wanted, dead or alive, damned near everywhere but here!"

Gaston nodded and said, *"Oui.* It is our own sweet young derrieres I am thinking of saving, Dick. We've enjoyed a most pleasant stay here in San José, but all in all, I think it is time we left for parts unknown again. It makes me nervous to have your Uncle Sam's undivided attention in any case. I don't think you were *diplomatique* in calling an embassy official a motherfucker, Dick. Whether we help the pretty German spy or not, I see no future for us here. We shall take her down to the coast and then double-cross her, *hein?"*

"What are you talking about? The deal was to convoy her down to the coast and back."

"Oui. So we shall only be half double-crossing her if we see her safely to Puntarenas. Whatever double-cross she may have in mind would be planned for the return trip. Meanwhile, since Puntarenas is a seaport . . ."

"Gotcha. Do we hop a freighter going north or south this time?"

"South, if we want work, and we'd best be thinking of

hiring out to someone or other before we run out of drinking money. I think we have just enough to book passage to Panama. That seems to be where the action is at the moment."

"I was afraid you'd say that," sighed Captain Gringo, adding, "Okay. If they can't use a machine-gun crew in Panama, they can't use one anywhere. Our next move is to get Claudette from her hotel to the stage station unobserved, which is . . . hmm, impossible."

"*Qui,* it might be best to double-cross her right off, *non?*"

"No. That won't work either. I already told her to meet us there in the morning. So she's bound to show up, with a brace of Secret Service agents tailing her. It gets worse. She's wired by now, so her pals in the seaport will be waiting for her. And said Secret Service will follow her all the goddamn way. Shit, there's got to be another way to skin this cat, Gaston!"

Gaston consulted his watch before he said, "I have skinned the cat many times, my old and rare. It is still too early. Four o'clock in the morning is the best time for skullduggery, *non?*"

"That's when cat burglars do it. If everyone's not asleep at that hour, forget it. But what's the plan?"

"*Eh bién,* if it's not obvious to you, how could the *très fatigué* Secret Service men forsee my brilliance, *hein?* In the eerie hours when only mice and ghosts come out to play, we shall sneak over to m'mselle's hotel and awaken her. At such an ungodly hour, who could be watching for her to make serious moves, *hein?*"

"Yeah, yeah, we can probably sneak her out of her hotel at four o'clock. But then what? There's nothing going on in San José at that hour."

"Exactly. The stage leaves just after dawn. No doubt the people watching her will be watching the stage station as well. But neither she nor the two of us leave on the stage for Puntarenas, won't they assume all three of us are simply late risers?"

"Sure. But how the hell are we supposed to get down to the coast if we don't board the coach, Gaston? It's too fucking far to walk, and it gets even worse once the sun comes up!"

"*Oui.* That is why nobody will expect us to try such a silly thing. We don't have to board the stage here in San José. It stops every six or seven miles. That is why they call it a stagecoach, *hein?* If we leave San José at four, we can easily be in Heredia by sunrise. Heredia is only two stages from here, *non?*"

"Hold it. That's twelve miles, and she's wearing high-heeled high-buttons. Can you get us a trio of burros?"

"But of course. I shall leave at once to pay a call on a rogue I know. I am sure he can supply us with mounts. But burros make such distressing hee-haws, so it would be best if I stayed well away from either hotel with them, *non?* Let me think. Ah, I shall have the burros ready in a safe place. I shall meet the two of you at Pedro's Smithy in the *barrio viejo.*"

"Gotcha," said Captain Gringo. He looked at his watch before he added, "I've still got time for forty winks if I set the alarm. I could use a bath, too. Take your stuff and one of these carbines so you don't have to come back, and make sure nobody follows you from this hotel, right?"

"*Merde alors,* Dick! Have you ever known me to be followed through dark alleyways far enough to be of any possible importance?"

Captain Gringo nodded, picked up his own carbine, and stuffed half the .38 rounds from the carton Claudette had given him in the side pocket of his jacket. Gaston was still gathering his own things as the younger man

37

left. He headed for the baths at the end of the hall before entering his own room. His bedroom bout with Claudette had left him feeling a little gamy, and a hot soak would do wonders for his bones, too. He was in good shape, but they'd overdone things a little back there, and he felt like he'd run a few miles. He grinned to himself as he ran the tub and stripped in the bath cubicle. At least he wasn't going to wake up with a hard-on in the foreseeable future!

But, it was a funny thing. As he settled his abused body in the comforting warmth of his bath, his damned fool tool responded to the luxurious tap water by twitching like an awakening monster. It got even harder when he carefully soaped it clean. He muttered, "I just want to make sure you don't get an infection, you silly little bastard. If we were jerking off I'd let you know."

The aroused, probably oversensitized creature seemed to have a mind of its own as he carefully made sure nothing naughty was imbedded in a pore or wrinkle. Sodomy in the tropics was as much fun as anywhere else. But a guy really had to worry about infection down here. And if there was one place he didn't want a tropic ulcer, his dong was it.

He got out and dried, trying to ignore the dumb erection. It was not only impossible but pointless at this hour. He dressed and returned to his room. As he unlocked the door, he saw by the light not shining from under the door next to his that Gaston had already left.

He ducked inside, then stiffened and reached for the .38 under his left armpit as he saw he was not alone in the room!

Then he relaxed as Maria switched on the bedlamp. His mestiza lay atop the sheets stark naked. It was warm, but not that warm, in San José at night. He started to ask her what the hell she was doing there, but that would have been a dumb question indeed, so he didn't. Maria smiled up at him and said, "Oh, *querido,* it is so late. I was afraid I would fall asleep before you came."

He said, "You're supposed to fall asleep *after* I come. Gaston didn't tell me you were here. What's up?"

"You, I hope. Gaston says the two of you are leaving town for a few days. Is this true, Deek?"

"Yeah, but we'll be coming right back," he lied. He felt shitty lying to such a sweet little thing. But peon girls threw such goddamn fits when you told them just to forget you that he'd given it up as a bad and sometimes dangerous habit.

As he slipped out of his clothes, Maria said, "Oh, I am so happy. You most obviously expected to find me here, no?"

He hadn't. But he didn't say so as he rolled atop her and she grasped his erection to guide it in. He wondered how the hell his pecker could have been expecting this ahead of him.

Maria had been waiting, expectantly, long enough to be almost crazy with desire as he lowered himself into the saddle of her tawny open thighs and let her put it in for him. She closed her eyes and crooned with delight as he did so. He kept his own eyes open to take in the delightful view as she gave herself to him. Her solid, almost stocky little brown body was such a contrast to Claudette's European build and whiter skin that he found, to his pleasant surprise, he seemed to be starting from scratch. Her firm brown breasts heaved up to meet his chest as she pulled him down on her and begged, "Kiss me, *por favor!* I wish to be kissed while I am climaxing!"

He kissed her. Her lips felt nothing like the lips he'd just left across town. Nothing about her felt the same. It was great. He repressed a chuckle as Maria tongued him passionately. He knew he should be feeling like a shit for having cheated on her. But there was something to be said for a change in partners. In truth, he'd been getting so much of little Maria of late that the dew had been fading from the old rose. Returning to her sweet, warm brown body after having another woman renewed his original enthusiasm and made him more aware of the simple charms that had first attracted him to her. So there was something to be said for musical beds, after all. No harm had been done and, in a way, all three of them had benefited from it.

But of course it took him forever to come again, even reinspired. Maria, bless her, took his prolonged effort for passion and was inspired to have repeated orgasms, which at least inspired him to keep going. He was tempted to fake it and call it a night. But he knew he'd probably never see Maria again and his old organ grinder would never forgive him if he abandoned ship after all this work. He raised himself on locked elbows again to stare down at himself as he slid in and out of her. Maria was writhing her hips from side to side and rolling her dark head back and forth across the pillow like a woman possessed, which she was, in a way. He was possessing her completely, but, damn, it sure was starting to seem more like work than pleasure. He didn't know how long he could keep it up. He decided to count to a hundred and quit, win place or draw. He knew he could thrust that many times, at least. But the sonofabitch was starting to go soft in her and he hadn't come once in her yet!

He got to thirty-seven when Maria stiffened in another orgasm, went limp, and gasped, "Have mercy, *querido!* I can't take any more! You have me so excited I can't stand it!"

By now he'd counted seventy-eight, and, what the hell, she'd asked him to stop. So what was he trying to prove? He gritted his teeth and went for an even hundred. As he got to ninety-five, Maria gasped in awe and groaned, "Maria, José y Jesus! It is happening again! Don't you Anglos know the meaning of enough?"

That reminded him again of Claudette, who qualified as Anglo down here, and so, between wanting to make sure Maria made it again, and remembering how different it had looked sliding in and out of the bigger white girl, Captain Gringo decided, what the hell, a hundred and *fifty* wouldn't kill him.

He didn't make it. As Maria wrapped her arms and legs around him again to hug him tightly against and in her, he suddenly, to his own surprise, exploded feebly in her. She crooned, "Oh, I felt that. It was so tightly pressed against the bottom when it spurted! But please don't do it again, Deek. You did not give me a chance to tell you. But I can't stay the night."

"Oh? What's wrong? Are you getting married in the morning?"

She started to cry. He kissed her and said, "Hey, I was just kidding."

"If only you were, Deek," she sighed, holding him tighter as she added, "If I tell you how wicked I have been, you will be most angry. But if I do not tell you, you will be so hurt, and I love you so much, my *querido!*"

He rolled off, fumbled a smoke from his shirt, and cuddled her head against his spare shoulder as he thumbed a match alight and lit his claro. He waited for her to get whatever was troubling her off her chest.

Her chest looked pretty good as Maria pulled away from him and sat up, naked, to start repinning her hair. He blew a thoughtful smoke ring. She looked away and said, "I had to come here, even knowing only wicked girls come to hotel rooms, when Gaston told me you'd be leaving. I was not going to tell you until this weekend, but Gaston says you may not be here."

"Okay, doll, so tell me now."

"I can't see you anymore, Deek. Today I got a letter from the prison. I was not expecting it to happen so soon. For so long I waited to get such a letter. But it never came, and then I met you, and, oh, Deek, I am so confused!"

He blew another smoke ring and said, "That makes two of us. Who's been in prison, Maria, some friend you're fond of?"

"Worse. It is my husband they had locked up these last three years. They said they were going to keep him in prison for five, but now they say they are letting him out early for good behavior, and, oh, *querido,* what are we to do?"

He smiled up at her wistfully and said, "Behave ourselves, I guess. If he's getting out next week, he'll sure as hell be expecting you to be waiting for him, right?"

"Yes, my *querido.* For a long time, when they took him away, I waited most faithfully for him. I think I may still love him. I know I loved him when they took him away. But now I love you, too. Do you think I am a wicked fickle-hearted *puta?*"

He reached out a hand to lay it on her thigh as he shook his head and said, "I think you're a human being, Maria. Three years is a long time."

"Oh, *madre mia,* that is all too true! I did not wish to fall in love with you, Deek. I only wished to . . ."

"Hey," he cut in, "don't punish yourself for having natural feelings, Maria. You're not a nun and God knows I've never acted like a priest. You don't have to explain to *me!*"

She turned to stare down at him, her doe eyes filled with childlike wonder, and asked, "Don't you feel like beating me, even a little bit, Deek?"

He said, "No. I'll settle for a goodbye kiss, *querida.*"

"Do you think we should, now that you know I am married?"

"Well, maybe you're right. At times like these we just have to rise above our natural feelings, right?"

Claudette was naked, too, when Captain Gringo woke her at four o'clock. She smiled up at him sleepily and asked, "What are you doing back here, darling? Didn't I give you enough loving for one night?"

He said, "No, but I'll survive. Get dressed, pronto. We're meeting Gaston and hopefully three burros. I'll explain it to you along the way."

He moved to the window as she sat up, stretching sensuously before asking what time it was. He said, "It's four in the morning and getting later by the second. Nobody tailed me from my place. I scouted the surrounding streets before slipping in here. As of now, nobody's down there holding up a lamp post with his Secret Service back. But time's awasting, honey."

She yawned, shook her head to clear it, then put a thoughtful hand between her thighs and said, "Hmm, I'm still hungry down here. Are you sure we don't have time for a quickie to wake me up, darling?"

"Later. We have to get out of town before anything or anybody else wakes up. Can you fit all your things in this big carpetbag. Claudette?"

"All the things I have to take with me. The rest can stay here till I get back. Can't we just do it one teeny weeny little time, darling? I don't know what you did to me before, but you seem to have created a monster."

"I noticed. I hope we haven't given each other a rash. Jesus Christ, you've taken your corset off?"

"Of course. You just noticed? I stripped completely after getting back from the *telegrafo*. How was I to know a sex-mad burglar would awaken me before dawn?"

She rose from the bed, long-limbed and silvery in the moonlight now that the street lamps had been snuffed out for the night. She picked up her corset, wrapped it about her waist, and turned her back to him as she braced herself against the washstand, saying, "You'll have to lace me up, lover. I'm too fumble-fingered at this ungodly hour."

He moved over and took the laces in hand to cinch her up as she bent over the washstand with her naked derriere to him, saying, "Tighter. There's no point to wearing the silly thing if it's loose as that!"

He pulled hard as she gripped the washstand with her hands. He got the corset tighter, but wound up with her bare butt against his pants.

She murmured, "Ooh, I can feel your dingdong through those thin tropical pants. *Do* it, Dick! Just whip it out and slip it in while you lace me up tighter!"

He had no intention of doing any such thing. But as he braced her bare buttocks against him to lace her right, Claudette reached back with one hand to fumble with his fly. He said, "Cut that out," and she said, "Oh, I *have* it out. But it's soft, the poor thing. Don't you like me anymore, Dick?"

He laughed and went on cinching her as she tried to get it in. It felt mighty interesting, but he knew she couldn't as long as it stayed limp. Then, as she somehow worked the head into her soft wet opening, he swore in mingled impatience and disbelief. The sonofabitch was starting to rise to the occasion again! But they didn't have time, and he knew he didn't have the lead in his pencil if there had been time. But as she arched her back and leaned back to swallow him deeper, he decided, what the hell, it didn't hurt. So he said, "Keep dressing. I've got you cinched. Here's your shift. Slip it on over your head, dammit."

"I've never heard of getting dressed to fuck, Dick." She giggled. But she seemed to enjoy the novelty as she started hauling on her things, bent over the stand with his shaft in her from behind. Her skirt had to stay up, of course. But by the time he had her bodice buttoned up the back, he was starting to enjoy the game too. So they got her shoes and stockings, then dropped to the floor on their knees, and, using a little ingenuity to keep it in, Claudette gartered her stockings and buttoned her shoes while he humped her. She came, or said she did. He couldn't. Not that way. But when he sat on the bed and told her to put her damned knickers on, Claudette did so while kneeling on the floor before him, squirming into her underwear as she finished him off with her mouth. And any man who couldn't come with Claudette blowing his whistle just wasn't alive enough to matter.

She laughed and wiped her lips off with a corner of the sheet as he recovered enough to groan, "I'll get you for that! But let's cut the bull and get out of here now. We've got some walking to do, if I'm still able to walk, you crazy bitch!"

He was able to walk, but just, as he led her down the back steps. The Winchester felt like it weighed as much as a field gun, and the loose ammo in his jacket tended to make him list to port. But as they went to meet Gaston he noticed that Claudette was still firm of foot and didn't seem to mind toting his valise as well as her own carpet-bag. He'd expected her to bitch when he told her he neeed one free hand. But she said she felt peppy as hell, now that she was fully awake.

Of course, she'd only screwed *one* person silly in the past twenty-four hours. He had to get out of San José before he was screwed to death. He felt weak as a kitten, which was only fair. Only a man in very good shape could have led her anywhere right now without at least a full twelve hours' bed rest. Alone.

She gazed up at the moon as she strode beside him, her high heels clicking on the flagstone paving. She said, "My, it's almost bright as day. How far is this place where we're meeting Gaston and the burros?"

"Less than half a mile. Could you walk a little less like castanets, doll? Those heels echo for at least two blocks."

"I thought you said everyone would be sleeping at this hour, dear."

"I know what I said. Let's try to *leave* them asleep as we pass, huh? What the hell have you got on those heels, metal taps?"

"Of course. Leather heels wear out in no time on the rough paving they have down here. Is this any better? I'm trying to walk on the balls of my feet."

He didn't answer as she went on click-clacking beside him. He couldn't expect her to tiptoe ten or twelve blocks packing two bags. They came to a corner and he stopped her while he scouted up and down the wider-than-average *calle* they had to cross. The street lamps were out, and nothing else seemed to be, either. He said, "Okay, we're coming to the *barrio viejo,* where half the dames go barefoot. I know the place Gaston's waiting with the burros, if he hasn't shacked up with one of those barefoot dames. So you'd better take those high-buttons off now, Claudette."

"Are you serious, Dick? I can't walk in my stocking feet, dammit!"

"Sure you can. It's the dry season and the dirt streets ahead are soft and dusty. Take off your stockings, too, if you're worried about stepping in horseshit."

She hesitated. He led her over to a door niche and sat her down on the high stone threshold, leaning the carbine against the stucco wall beside her as he said, "Come on. It's getting later by the minute and we have to make some silent tracks. I'll help you."

46

He dropped to one knee and began to unbutton one of her shoes as she giggled and said, "You look like you're about to go down on me."

He growled, "Jesus, don't you ever think of anything else?"

She gasped, "Dick! Look out!" And then the roof fell in on him!

There were two of them, as far as he could tell when they flattened him on the pavement in front of the seated girl. Where they'd come from and who they were was less important at the moment than the fact that they had him on the bottom and would have been hurting him even more if they hadn't gotten in each other's way as they both tried to beat him up at once!

His shoulder rig was under all three of them as he tried in vain to reach across his chest, pressed to the pavement while some sonofabitch had him by the hair and was trying to flatten his face by pounding it on the ground. A fortunately bare foot slammed into his ribs as he realized there were at least three of the bastards, and what the hell was he supposed to do about it?

Then the pressure eased, just enough, when Claudette sprang up, silent as a mouser, to swing her heavy carpet-bag with all her might against the head of the nearest attacker! It rolled him half off Captain Gringo. It was just enough to allow the big Yank to roll on his left shoulder and get at his gun. The guy who'd been kicking him went for Claudette as she braced her back against the door behind her, trying to fend him off with the bags in both hands. Captain Gringo rolled over farther, back-handing the guy atop his upper body across the face with his gun barrel.

That took care of one. There was another prick perched on his lap. So Captain Gringo shot his face off, and sat up in time to see the glint of moonlight on steel in the nearby doorway. But Claudette was thinking fast, too, and

47

as he slashed at her she caught his blade with her carpet-bag. Then Captain Gringo blew him away from her with a bullet in his kidney.

That made it two down and one to go. As Captain Gringo rose to one knee, he saw that the thug he'd pistol-whipped off him had recovered enough to stagger over to the carbine leaning against the wall, and, even as Captain Gringo aimed at him, the Winchester's muzzle flashed in his face!

Captain Gringo returned the fire, nailing the guy over the heart as he wondered, dully, how come he was still alive. But there wasn't time to pinch himself.

He leaped up, snapped, "Follow me!" and hung around just long enough to pick up the still-warm Winchester before heading across the broad *calle* as, behind him, dogs barked, doors opened, and Claudette still click-clacked like castanets. But at least he knew she was still with him. And when he turned to look back toward the safety of the shadows on the far side, he saw that she still had both their bags, God bless her. He could always get more gear. But it was bad enough he'd left his hat behind for the cops to have a look at when they arrived.

She was breathing heavily as she caught up with him. She asked, "What happened? Who were those men? Why are we stopping?"

He looked around, grabbed her by an elbow, and steered her into a dark narrow slot between two patioed houses. The little passageway between blank walls smelled of stale piss, but, as he'd hoped, a slit of light at the far end showed it led clean through to another street. He said, "As I was saying before we were so rudely interrupted, take off those fucking high heels!"

He holstered his .38, dropped to one knee, and pulled off the shoe he'd just unbuttoned when they'd jumped him. As he was taking off the other, she asked again, "Who on earth were they, Dick?"

He said, "Don't know. They might have been after me. They might have been after you. They might have just been thugs out to rob anyone dumb enough to be out on the streets at this hour. It's a good thing they didn't start out with their own guns."

"Brrr! I saw! I thought you were dead when he fired that carbine at you back there, dear!"

"I thought I was too. The more I think about it, the more it looks like they were just *ladróns*. They were dressed like peons, and nobody misses with a long gun at such close range unless he's never had much practice. They probably heard those damned heels, took us for a couple of sweethearts coming home late, and figured they could take us with just knives and fists."

He straightened up, holding her shoes, and added with a grimace, "Come to think of it, one of 'em kicked pretty good. I feel great in the small of my back. Remind me never to get kicked there again after a night of hard screwing. Put these in my bag. There's plenty of room."

A police whistle sounded in the distance. Claudette gasped and said, "Oh, we have to run!" but he said, "Only chumps run when people are looking out their windows at a noisy street, doll. Come on, we ease out the far end, like we've been tearing off a wall job in here, then we stroll, arm in arm, and . . . damn, who ever heard of strolling arm in arm with a lady of the evening while packing a Winchester?"

"Can't we sort of hold it between us, dear? We can't leave it behind."

He thought, then said, "Sure we can. I'll just put it down right here and the first kid cutting through in the morning will make sure the cops never find it."

As he leaned the Winchester against a wall, Claudette said, "But, Dick, we need that for later, on the stage!"

He took her elbow to lead her out of the slot, saying, "Gaston still has one long gun and we're both packing pissolivers. I know what you're thinking, doll. But you have to think faster, in our line of work. The idea is to get you down to Puntarenas unobserved. People observe the shit out of heavily armed travelers."

"But the bandits, on the coach road . . ."

"The odds are we won't meet any bandits. But we're sure to pass more than one lawman on the Puntarenas Trail. The Costa Ricans worry about bandits, too. They patrol the roads a lot with mounted troopers, see?"

She didn't argue. All hell seemed to be breaking loose over on the far side of the broad *calle*. But nobody seemed to give a damn on the narrow side street they were on as he led her down it, silent in her stocking feet.

Gaston was waiting for them in front of the smithy. He was alone. He said, *"Eh bien,* it's about time you got here. What happened to your hat, Dick?"

A rooster crowed in the distance. So Captain Gringo said. "It's a long story. Let's get the hell out of here. Where are the burros?"

"In the corral, out back. *Merde alors,* have you lost your carbine, too?"

"I said it was a long story, dammit. I'll tell you about it on the trail to Heredia. Would it make you move any faster if I told you we just left three bodies and half the cops in town less than a mile from here?"

Gaston whistled under his breath and took the lead. As he led them around the apparently deserted smithy he confided, "Pedro is awake inside. He said he did not wish to get involved. We're to leave his burros with a kinsman in Heredia. That's all he wants to know about our business."

Captain Gringo muttered, "Good old Pedro." But then he spotted the three mounts waiting for them in the moonlight behind the smithy and growled, "I'll get the bastard for this! Are those things supposed to be burros? They look like coyotes. Small ones!"

"I told him his mother and sisters are all whores, Dick. He still said these were all he had. But consider the alternatives, *hein?* Even a baby burro beats walking."

The three burros did beat walking. Just. Even the shorter Gaston's boot tips scraped the ground if he let them as they rode out together. Claudette, riding side-saddle, had better luck. They'd let her put her shoes back on and her toes cleared the road by about a foot. Captain Gringo had to bend his knees a lot to keep from walking in step with his little mount as he rode it. He could have walked faster. He would have been tempted to, if he hadn't been so tired and Heredia had been a little closer.

The sky was already getting lighter as they left the outskirts of San José. By then he'd brought Gaston up to date on the street fight. When he praised Claudette's own fighting skills with a carpetbag, Gaston frowned and turned to look back thoughtfully at the blonde, saying, "I admire savage women, m'mselle. But I find it curious that such an adventuress does not carry a gun of her own. Does not it make you nervous to lead such an active life without so much as a derringer in your possession?"

She said, "I've always been afraid of guns. I know it's silly, but I can't help it. I've only fired a gun once or twice in my life, and I've never been able to hit anything. The noise makes me flinch."

Captain Gringo chuckled wryly and said, "Drop it, Gaston. She's got other weapons to fall back on in a pinch."

Considering how complicated life had been up to now, things went smooth as silk in the little town of Heredia. It was just waking up as they rode in. But nobody seemed curious enough to bother them. Gaston left them by the stage stop while he got rid of the burros. The arcaded two-story building included a one-table café that had just opened. So they ordered coffee. The fat, mustached woman who served them was still half-asleep and didn't seem interested in what they were doing in her place so early in the morning. Gaston joined them and had coffee, too, as they waited for the stage from San José. Their luck held out. The mule-drawn stage arrived on time, and the only other passenger was a little old lady in a rusty black dress who didn't take up enough room to matter. The jehu and his shotgun rider took their *dinero* and told them to pile aboard. They didn't even ask why Gaston was packing a carbine.

That was something to think about as the stage rolled out of Heredia. Maybe there had been talk of bandits on the trail, after all. Captain Gringo decided he'd better stay awake as he sat by the right-hand window, facing backward, while Gaston of course faced forward, with his carbine braced out the sloping sill of the left-hand window on his side. The two women sat across from each other on the facing seats The old lady rode facing forward while Claudette shared her seat with Captain Gringo. As the mules trotted monotonously ahead of them, Claudette engaged the old woman in conversation, bless her. Captain Gringo and Gaston could tell the blonde was pumping the sweet old thing, but the woman who'd ridden the stage out of San José didn't know that. Claudette was soon able to establish that, yes, there had been another awful street crime back in San José and, no, the police had no idea who'd shot those three unfortunates in the wee small hours. The old woman said, *"Los pobrecitos* are always killing one another at night around the *barrio viejo.* I was told one of the men killed last night had a reputation for violence. It is thought it was a gang fight."

Captain Gringo restrained himself, and, sure enough, Claudette was smart enough to ask, very casually, "Oh? Don't the police have any idea who might have done it?"

The old woman sighed and said, "No. I do not think they care. None of the dead men were of any importance. As I said, the poor brutes are always fighting among themselves, and as long as nobody wearing shoes was hurt, perhaps the whole disgusting affair can be forgotten.

Captain Gringo nudged Claudette's ankle with his own to shut her up. She'd asked enough and it was time to change the subject. He knew that one of the first arrivals on the scene had helped himself to the lost hat and had doubtless been wearing it when the police arrived. The cops would never see the carbine he'd left in the alley slot, either, so what the hell.

Claudette either figured all that out herself or just took nudges well, because she changed the subject to the small talk about cooking and sewing that women indulged in instead of sports. He was glad she was handling the old woman so well. But he saw it was sure going to be a long, dull trip.

It was, for a while. An hour after setting out, they stopped at some dinky town to change mules and drink some more coffee. Neither helped a hell of alot. The trail was still uphill, so even fresh mules moved less than six miles an hour, and Captain Gringo could have jogged along beside the coach and likely passed it with a little effort. And the coffee didn't do that much good for him. He was in no shape for jogging, walking, or even keeping his eyes open for God's sake. He wondered dully how Claudette could sound so bright-eyed and bushy-tailed as she chatted on and on with the old lady about nothing much. He knew she'd been on the bottom most of the time, and that side trip to Maria's brown body had only been rough on *him*. But it still didn't seem fair. Whoever had first declared that women were the weaker sex couldn't have laid many of them in his time.

He rubbed a hand across his face. It didn't help. He was watching the downhill side now as the trail swung around a higher rise. Nobody was going to lope a pony up such a grade at them. Gaston and the shotgun rider, topside, were doubtless watching the uphill side. So what was he trying to prove? Would it kill him if he closed his damned eyes and just went with the feeling?

It probably would, as he'd learned the hard way in times past. He shook his head to clear it and sat straighter in his swaying seat. He'd sleep when they got to Puntarenas. Boy, would he sleep when they got to Puntarenas!

But he was dozing off again, despite himself, when Gaston suddenly yelled, *"Regardez!* Up the slope ahead!" and fired his carbine out the windows of his side.

Captain Gringo's pistol was out of its shoulder holster before his eyes were open. But when he stared out his side, there was nothing much going on. Then a distant rifle spanged, and the body of the shotgun rider fell limply past his window to land like a sack of potatoes on the shoulder of the trail, rolling down the slope, flopping limp dead arms and legs as it just kept rolling. Captain Gringo yelled, "Down, Claudette! Take care of the other lady, too!" as he rolled over her to the uphill side. He got to the window next to Gaston's as the little Frenchman fired again. He didn't ask questions. He could see the sonsofbitches among the rocks up there now!

There were at least a dozen, though it was hard to tell just how many were hidden. The wily bastards had left their mounts on the far side of the ridge and hunkered down among the trailside boulders to ambush the stage. And they were ambushing it pretty good!

He could tell by the way they were rolling that the driver had let go of the reins and the spooked mules were bolting, paying no mind to the ruts and bumps as they dragged the coach wildly after them at a dead run. Captain Gringo knew they could all wind up dead if somebody didn't control the runaway team pronto. He fired his pistol at a big hat aiming a rifle over a rock at him, then kicked open the door and yelled, "Cover me, Gaston!"

Captain Gringo didn't wait for an answer. He was too busy climbing up the side of the sickeningly swaying stagecoach as Gaston fired round after round out the window below. As Captain Gringo swung up into the boot to find the driver's seat blood-smeared and vacant, a bullet tore slivers out of the wood between his legs, close enough to sting his balls. He clung to the brass baggage rail with one hand, firing his pistol with the other, and yelled down, "God damn it! I asked you to *cover* me, you blind ass Frog!"

Gaston yelled back, "I can't shoot through rocks, *merde alors,* and this triple-titted coach will tip over if you don't *do* something soon!"

Captain Gringo ignored a bullet whizzing by his ear as he looked down in the boot for some trace of the reins. There weren't any. The damned driver had dropped them when he'd been blasted off his seat. They were trailing in the dust between the mules ahead, and the mules were almost to the top of a rise. If they were going this fast uphill, they'd be going a lot faster down the far side, and the damned fool mules didn't know that an unbraked heavy coach would overtake them and wind up in a hell of a tangled mess, *muy pronto!*

Captain Gringo holstered his .38 and grabbed the brake handle with both fists. He locked the wheels with no trouble. But it didn't slow the mules enough to matter. If he dropped down between them to retrieve the reins, he'd have to let go of the brake. Another bandit bullet made his mind up for him by thudding into the leather cushion an inch from his ass and spraying him with horse-hair stuffing. He said, "Oh, shit," and let go of the brake.

The coach of course leaped forward again as he dropped over the dashboard between the rumps of the rear mules. One foot missed the wagon tongue. The other didn't. So, by kneeling between the sweaty mules, groping in the dusty confusion with one hand and hanging on to the harness with the other, Captain Gringo managed to gather the loose reins. Another bullet tore splinters off the dashboard as he forked himself back up into the driver's seat. He braced himself with one heel against the dash to haul in on the reins. He got his other heel against the brake rod and shoved hard. But not too hard. The idea was to slow down enough to keep from turning over, not to come to a dead stop in the middle of a bandit fusillade!

It seemed to be working. They topped the rise and were out of range by the time he had the team under control again. He looked back and saw a guy in a big hat waving a fist at them as they went over the rise. He sighed and muttered, "Up yours, too! Okay, mules, you've had your romp, and it's all downhill to the next stage. So behave yourselves, dammit!"

They did. They trotted sedately ahead, relieved of their burden as he controlled the downhill roll of the heavy coach with his boot on the brake handle. They'd gone maybe half a mile when Gaston climbed up to join him, saying, "*Sacrebleu* that was *très* noisy back there, *non?* Where are the people who usually ride up here, Dick?"

"Back with the *banditos*. Hopefully, feeling no pain. When we get to the next stage, we'll tell 'em what happened and let *them* worry about it. Are the women all right?"

"*Oui*. Both alive and well by some miracle. Considering how much lead they were throwing back there, I am overjoyed to see you looking so well, too."

"They aimed first at the crew. I doubt if they expected the team to bolt on an uphill grade. Did you hit anything but rocks back there?"

Gaston shrugged and asked, "Who looks behind rocks at such a time? I emptied this carbine at them and my pistol, too. If I didn't hit anyone, I certainly made them duck, *non?*"

"Yeah, I think I emptied my .38 at 'em, too," said Captain Gringo, letting go with one hand long enough to draw his revolver and hand it to Gaston as he added, "Check it for me, will you? I may need a reload."

Gaston broke the .38 open and said, "You do, you noisy child. I still have plenty of spares in my pocket. I have already reloaded. Reloaded my pistol, that is. M'mselle Claudette says there are no spare .44-40s in her adorable carpetbag."

Captain Gringo frowned as he watched the slopes on either side and went on driving. He said, "That's stupid. Why did she buy two carbines without picking up extra ammo, dammit?"

"Ask her. She said she was unfamiliar with guns, as I recall. But at least we have plenty of pistol rounds. Here, yours is loaded, so put it away. Perhaps we can pick up carbine ammunition in the next town, *non?*"

Captain Gringo reholstered his sidearm as he thought about that. Then he said, "I've got a better idea."

He called down to Claudette and, when she stuck out her blond head, told her, "Toss that Winchester over the side, doll. There's no point answering questions about a goddamn gun nobody can shoot!"

The conversation was in English, of course. The other passenger might or might not ask Claudette why the useless carbine had gone out the window to land in some cactus. Gaston had that part figured out, but asked, "What if we run into more bandits, Dick?"

Captain Gringo shrugged and said, "We'll have to make do with our only loaded guns, of course. We're going to be stuck in the next town awhile. They'll probably send

57

us on with an armed escort, if they don't arrest us. The fewer odd questions we have to answer, the less chance they'll be suspicious, right?"

"*Oui*, but this certainly is not the way I would have chosen to slip into Puntarenas without attracting notice, Dick."

They were noticed indeed, but not arrested, when Captain Gringo drove into the yard of the next stage stop. As he'd foreseen, they were held up a good two hours while the local *alcalde* sent for the guard and the coach company sent a buckboard back up the trail for the bodies.

The dead driver and his shotgun rider were laid out in the stable of the local coroner and carpenter by the time a corporal's squad of mounted guardsmen rode in. The young noncom in command looked intelligent, God damn him. He told the travelers to wait in the cantina while he had a look at the dead men. He took his own sweet time. When he rejoined them, he asked to see their weapons.

The two soldiers of fortune had no choice but to hand over their pistols. The corporal had noticed they were Anglos, or assumed they were, and spoke English to be courteous as he handed their guns back with a smile, saying, "Forgive my curiosity, señores. While I never doubted your story for a moment, I had to make sure. The stagecoach crew were shot with rifles. You caballeros are only armed with pistols. The matter is settled to my satisfaction. As soon as a fresh team and the new crew is ready to proceed, my men and I will make sure you get down out of these rough hills unmolested. We can only escort you as far as Orobina. But from there to Puntarenas our country is well settled by much nicer people, so you should have no further trouble."

58

Captain Gringo invited him and his troopers to join them for some cerveza. He didn't have to twist any arms. So by the time the coach was ready to go on, they were all pals. But Captain Gringo stayed awake, anyway, as he once more rode below with the others. The unexpected excitement had given him his second wind. He knew his muscles were going to ache for the next few days, whether he got any sleep or not. But he could keep his eyes open now.

He kept his ears open, too, as he listened to the two women chat on as if nothing had happened. The nice old lady had apparently been on the bottom with Claudette shielding her during the gun battle back there. If she'd wondered, or even noticed, that Gaston had started out with a carbine and wound up with a pistol, she didn't drop so much as a veiled hint about it. He was braced for her to mention a relative who needed an operation. But the sweet old thing just didn't seem to know she was in position to shake them down.

He told himself he was getting mighty suspicious in his old age. On the other hand, he'd been double-crossed more than once by even nicer-looking people. If *he* wanted to get old, he knew he had to suspect even sweet old ladies.

Gaston's mind, being even older, seemed to be running in the same channels as he sat facing Captain Gringo, wearing a slight frosty smile. In English, he said casually, "When one was there, one would see no reason to wonder if one of us went mad and shot the crew, *non?*"

"Knock it off. I've already doped that out. And it's not polite to speak English in front of a lady I hope only speaks Spanish."

"I checked that out, too," said Gaston, switching back to Spanish to add, "It seems to be getting warmer as we drop to a lower altitude, don't you agree?"

It wasn't getting warmer. It was starting to get hot as

hell. At least they were making up for lost time. The new crew, no doubt uneasy about bandits even with an escort, took advantage of the downhill grade and fresh mules. But it still took a hell of a long time to get to the end of the line. The corporal and his men turned back to ride back up into the cooler hills, once they were passing bananas, peppers, and other hothouse plants on either side. By the time they reached Puntarenas they all looked and felt like they'd spent half the day in a Turkish steam-bath. But they finally made it, late that afternoon. Better yet, nobody seemed at all interested as they stiffly climbed down from the coach, said adios to the crew and old lady, and headed for a no-questions hotel Gaston naturally knew about.

Like most hotels of the time and place, this one had the coeducational bathroom down at the end of the hall. Since women and children went first, Claudette staggered down to wash and cool her flushed flesh, thus leaving the two soldiers of fortune alone for the moment.

Captain Gringo muttered, "Jesus, what a dump," as he started to take off his jacket.

Gaston said, "Don't undress. We'll never have a better opportunity to, how you say, ditch that blonde, *hein?*"

Captain Gringo stared dully at him and said, "I'm too pooped to run anymore in this heat, Gaston. Besides, I'm curious. We have to scout the waterfront in any case. Why not tag along to her meeting at the waterfront cantina and see what happens?"

Gaston rolled his eyes heavenward and replied, "Why not just put your .38 to your thick skull and pull the trigger? I only brought us here because I did not wish her to know about the much nicer place we can hide out until I can arrange passage out of here, Dick. We know why she is going to meet someone down on the docks later this evening. She is a spy. They are spies. Spies make me *très* nervous, even when they are not Germans.

German spies are even worse. I think it must be all that sour food they eat that gives them such acid dispositions, *non?*"

Captain Gringo took off his jacket and sat on the bed. Gaston asked, "Have you wax in your ears? *Merde alors,* let's get out of here! What are you waiting for?"

Captain Gringo said, "I'm thinking. You said there was a fifty-fifty chance we could hop a freighter out of here without getting nailed, right?"

"Oui, if we start searching for safe passage soon."

"That's what I thought you said. That means there's a fifty-fifty chance we *won't* make it! Those are piss-poor odds when you consider the table stakes, Gaston!"

"True. But it seems to be the only game in town, *non?"*

"That's what I'm thinking about. Claudette's some kind of secret agent. But so far she seems to be on our side. She has contacts here and money waiting for her back in San José. I think she likes me. She sure swings a mean carpetbag when guys sit on my head."

Gaston snorted in disgust and said, "She was saving herself as well. The woman is an adventuress who works for the highest bidder. Why should she share her payoff with us, and even if she likes you that much, how could we possibly go back to San José with her to get it now?"

Captain Gringo shook his head stubbornly and said, "I can't think of a place those embassy guys would expect to see me *least.* By now they must know all three of us are no longer to be found up in San José. Ergo, that's the last place they'll expect to see us. We could hide out with your pals in the *barrio viejo* till the heat died down. Then, with the payoff old Claudette promised, we could walk, not run, for the nearest exit that no damned bounty hunter is watching."

Gaston started to object. Then he sighed and said, "Far be it from me to discuss doubling back on one's trail with a fellow fox. It is so risky-sounding it may just work, with one big *if*. At the moment, m'mselle If is taking a bath down the hall, *hein?*"

Captain Gringo nodded and said, "I've considered all the ways she could be plotting to double-cross us. She's a spy, not a bounty huntress. The accumulated rewards outstanding on the two of us add up to more than the people she's working for will pay her for delivering her emeralds, secret plans, or whatever. But she would have turned us in by now if that had been her game. She spotted me before I spotted her, remember?"

Claudette came back in, wearing just a towel. Gaston nodded politely and said, "Ah, we were just talking about you, m'mselle."

Claudette threw herself face down across the bed and said, "It didn't work. I'm too exhausted to think straight. If either of you mean to fuck me, please don't wake me up before sundown."

The two soldiers of fortune looked at each other and laughed. Gaston said, *"Eh bien,* I will flip you to see who goes to take a bath and who stays here, *hein?"*

Captain Gringo said, "We're both going to leave her alone in here, for now. We booked adjoining rooms, if you want to call these rooms. Come on. You can hit the tub. I'll lock her in and stand guard next door."

Gaston muttered, "Spoilsport!" but allowed himself to be ushered out to the hall as Captain Gringo locked the door. Gaston said, "You go ahead and bathe. You look red as a lobster and I do not think it's maidenly modesty. You may be suffering heat stroke, Dick. I'm serious. I know the signs. Go soak yourself in cool water until your skin looks human again. Never fear for your place in line, my suspicious youth. I know when a woman means it and when she is only showing off."

Captain Gringo didn't argue. He really did feel lousy. As he headed for the bath at the end of the hall, the floor rolled under him like the deck of a ship at sea. He felt like he had to throw up, too. But he didn't. He put his head down against his knees while the tub filled, and that helped. The cool soak helped even more. He felt so much better by the time he climbed out that he knew Gaston had been right and he'd just had a brush with the real thing. He'd thought he was too enured to the tropics by now to suffer heat stroke like a greenhorn. But coming down from the highlands so suddenly after beating himself up with more sex than any man really needed had apparently lowered his resistance.

He relieved Gaston. He sat on the bed in the empty room with the hall door open while the Frenchman cooled his own flesh. By the time Gaston got back, Captain Gringo felt like he needed another bath. He said, "Jesus, I'm sweating like a pig. How hot do you think it is outside right now?"

"Don't ask. It's hot enough in here! It will soon begin to cool off. But you had better take a nap, Dick. I can stand guard over you children. I was not dumb enough to clamber over thundering stagecoaches after street fights and astounding orgies, *hein?*"

Captain Gringo flopped on the bed, still dressed, and said, "When you're right you're right. But who said I had any astounding orgies?"

"You did, when you didn't even notice her derriere as she exposed it falling down in the next room. No man born of mortal woman fails to blink at a derriere like that unless he's had so much of it he can't take another bite. Besides, I left Maria waiting for you last night at our hotel, and I did not hear her screaming, as she would have, if you hadn't taken time to comfort her before you left."

Captain Gringo chuckled as he closed his eyes and muttered, "Old Maria told me she's married. Ain't that a pisser?"

"*Oui.* But I can't say I find it surprising. You went with her nearly a month, you know. I've never met a woman who fails to insist on marriage within a month, unless she has some greater treachery in mind for her victim."

Sleeping alone, for however short a time, did wonders for both Captain Gringo and Claudette. They were both able to walk without staggering as all three of them went over to the waterfront at sundown. They ordered food as well as drinks at the sidewalk cantina facing the quay. Claudette had said that the owner of the joint was a contact, but nobody there acted like they'd ever seen her before. Apparently *Der Kaiser* paid well.

As they lounged under the awning, watching the harbor, the red sunset etched the boats out on the water in black outlines. Captain Gringo saw one was a squat gunboat, but he couldn't make out its colors against the sunset. He commented on the fact that someone was being diplomatic to Costa Rica, too. But Claudette said, "The vessel we have to worry about is one of those four schooners. I don't see anyone lowering a longboat. Do you?"

Captain Gringo squinted and said, "No. It's early yet. The light's shining on us from where they sit out there on the water. If anyone's expecting you, they've spotted you by now."

He ate some more tacos con refritos. They tasted awful. His cerveza tasted lousy too. But he didn't blame the cook inside. He knew he was still sick.

Gaston was questioning Claudette again, about their payoff back up in San José. Captain Gringo wished he'd shut up. That part of the deal was not the problem. The problem was picking up whatever, here, and seeing that Claudette got safely with it to the French syndicate she said she was working for, the German embassy Carson had said she was working for, or whoever the hell she *was*

64

working for. Going back by stage was too obvious. Walking was too fatiguing. He felt too lousy to think about it right now. They'd worry about it later, after a good night's sleep.

Gaston said, *"Regardez!* A boat is coming in. It seems to be a power launch."

Captain Gringo squinted out across the harbor, and, sure enough, a low steam launch had popped out from somewhere and was moving their way under its little smoke plume. He could make out figures under the full-length canopy running from stem to stern, but he couldn't count how many there were.

Someone aboard the launch struck a match or blinked a flashlight on and off. Claudette said, "That's our signal," and got to her feet.

Gaston muttered, "What does she mean, *our* signal?" But when Captain Gringo rose to follow her, Gaston got up too.

The three walked to the edge of the quay as the steam launch nudged its fendered bow against the sea wall. A man called out, "M'mselle Pardeau?" and Claudette called back, *"Oui* Do you have my package?"

A couple of seamen leaped ashore with a painter to steady the launch as the man under the awning replied, "Not here. Out on the vessel. Get aboard, all three of you, quickly. Before we're noticed."

Claudette moved forward. But Captain Gringo grabbed her arm and said, "Hold it, kiddies! My mama once told me never to do things the complicated way when the best way looks simple!"

Claudette said, "It's all right, Dick. I know them."

He said, "But I don't. How come you want us to pick up out there, when you could have just brought it in with you?"

He never heard or saw the signal. But there must have been one, because one of the seamen who'd jumped up

65

on the quay with them suddenly rabbit-punched Captain Gringo from behind and sent him sprawling forward into the bow of the launch.

He landed on his side, dazed, but still able to draw as he gasped, "Gaston! It's a trap!" then fired up into the men above him, double-action, until his hammer was clicking in frustration as they all seemed intent on kicking him at once. He tried to rise as he heard Gaston's gun go off.

Then Gaston landed on top of him, out like a light with a nasty bump over the left ear. It broke Gaston's fall to land atop Captain Gringo. But it didn't make Captain Gringo feel any better. Somebody flattened him on his back with a boot planted in the center of his chest, and as he stared up into the muzzle of a twelve-gauge riot gun, a voice he'd heard before said, in English, "Okay, cut the bullshit, Walker. *This* gun happens to be loaded! We want you alive. But don't push your luck, renegade!"

Captain Gringo could only curse as they hauled him to a seated position and cuffed his hands behind him while Gaston lay unconscious across his legs. He spotted Claudette wistfully looking down at him from the quay above and yelled, "You bitch! I trusted you!"

She said, "A girl has to live, dear." Then she waved bye-bye with her hankie as the steam launch backed off to take him and Gaston out to the gunboat moored offshore.

As they approached an angle that let him see her colors better, he wasn't at all surprised to see the Stars and Stripes. He looked up at the man with the shotgun and growled, "Nice going, Carson. I take it you're not with the State Department after all?"

Carson smiled down thinly at him as another seaman knelt to cuff the unconscious Gaston. Carson said, "U.S. Navy Intelligence, doing a favor for War. It's the least we could do after you suckered our marines in Venezuela that time."

Gaston groaned and tried to sit up, asking where he was. Captain Gringo said, "You're on my lap, wearing cuffs behind you. We seem to be guests of the U.S. Navy."

Gaston rolled off, managed to sit up, and blinked around owlishly as he took in his new surroundings. He said, *"Merde alors,* I knew they had ironclad gunboats, but ironclad *sailors,* too?"

Captain Gringo said, "I heard you shooting, pard. You can thank sweet Claudette for those sneaky bullets. How did those blanks work, Carson? Lead foil over wadding?"

Carson smiled smugly and said, "You're learning. Navy Ordinance can make anything. The Winchesters we provided were loaded with harmless ammo, too."

"I figured as much. It was pretty shitty of you to blow away those poor Costa Ricans just to get us to expend all our real ammo, Carson. I don't suppose you'd want to have me mention that at my trial back in the States, huh?"

"What trial?" Carson gloated, adding, "You already had your trial, Walker. You were sentenced to hang before you escaped from that army guardhouse. We're just taking you back and turning you over to the army so they can carry out the sentence!"

"That sounds reasonable. But what about my buddy here? He's never stood trial in the States, yet."

"Don't worry about it, Walker. Mon-sewer Verrier has sure been tried in absentia in Mexico. We'll be dropping him off at Mazatlán when we put in there on a goodwill mission."

"You prick! You smug fucking chickenshit! You killed two innocent guys just so you could say you took us alive, right?"

"Those were my orders, Walker. I don't suppose a

renegade like you would understand that orders are meant to be carried out to the letter."

Captain Gringo watched the oncoming stern of the gunboat as he shook his head and said, "When you're right, you're right. I've never understood pricks like you and I hope I never will. Sure, I can see a guy doing his job. But the wants on us are dead or alive. You went to all that trouble, razzle-dazzle and murder, just to take us alive so some *other* pricks can hang us?"

"That's right, Walker. And I'm pleased as punch everything went so well. Don't try to understand me, Walker. You won't live long enough to figure all the moves I made."

By the time the two soldiers of fortune were locked alone together in the hold, they'd learned that Carson was a lieutenant J.G. and that the other guys aboard the gunboat weren't such bastards. The U.S. Navy didn't pay enough to attract many really dedicated bastards like Carson.

The skipper, an older officer whose name they didn't catch, ordered their cuffs removed once they were safely locked below. Carson was in charge only of them, not of the gunboat. It had been his idea to lock them in an empty ammo locker under the stern guns, where the vibrations of the screw could shake the shit out of them every time they topped a ground swell. The locker had never been intended as a brig, so there were no sanitary facilities. A crewman issued them blankets to spread on the riveted steel deck. He said he was sorry the deck was wet. The gunboat was old, Washington was on yet another economy drive, and, aside from being low on food and ammo, the old tub leaked a lot.

A new door of boiler plate had been fitted in advance

on Carson's orders It was solider than the somewhat rusty side plates of the vessel and the prick had seen to it that the padlock couldn't be reached from inside.

Captain Gringo spread his blankets on the wet steel deck and went to sleep for a million years. He had some really lousy dreams. But when he woke up he said he felt better. Gaston said it was no wonder, as he'd slept around the clock. He added, "I hope you don't mind my eating your food as well as mine. Lieutenant Carson is *très fatigue*, but the enlisted men seem decent enough. I extended my compliments to the chef. The food aboard is quite reasonable."

Captain Gringo sat up, moving his back when he felt a trickle of sea water running down his spine from a sprung rivet. He rubbed a hand across the stubble on his jaw and asked, "What time is it?" Then as he stared up at the little barred opening in the door, he asked, "What the fuck is *that?*"

Gaston followed his gaze and smiled crookedly at the little hangman's noose someone had improvised with twine to sway just outside the bars. Gaston said, "I told you Lieutenant Carson was *très fatigue*."

He snapped another card down on the wet deck between his legs, and for the first time Captain Gringo saw he was playing solitaire. He asked Gaston where he'd gotten the cards and Gaston said, "From a rather pleasant Yankee seaman. They took everything we had in our pockets, as you know, but I was able to convince him that playing cards are hardly deadly weapons, and he agreed it was improper for a man my age to jack off all the way to Mazatlán."

Captain Gringo moved again and muttered, "We may not get that far in this tub. We seem to be just about at the waterline, and the water's coming in a lot!"

"*Oui*, from the way the plates are rusted, under the surface neatness of that last paint job. I would say waterline is midway up the bulkhead. Hopefully, the pumps below us can deal with the leakage for now. Once we arrive in Mexico, I really don't care if she sinks or not."

"Gee, thanks. They're taking me on to San Diego!"

"Do you really care if you get back there or not, Dick?"

Captain Gringo grimaced and said, "Guess not. Drowning can't feel much worse than hanging. I'm sorry, Gaston. We wouldn't be in this fix if I'd listened to you back there."

Gaston shrugged and said, "*Merde alors,* they would have picked us up in any case, once they had the machinery in gear. Has it occurred to you we were on their hook from the first, my guilt-ridden youth?"

Captain Gringo shook his head and said, "Carson must be so pleased with himself that he's coming in his pants. Boy, to think I fell for his yarn about being from the embassy! They had to get us down to the coast to nail us, and I thought I was being so damned smart as they reeled us in!"

There was a clatter of steel on steel and the door opened to let a seaman in with a tray. A pistol-packing C.P.O. stood behind him, just in case, so neither prisoner moved as the seaman put the tray down near them. He said, "Sorry about that dumb noose out there, guys. It wasn't our idea."

Gaston said, "We know, *mon ami.* But listen, could you possibly get us another deck of cards?"

"How come? How many cards do you *need,* for chrissake?"

"Fifty-two, if we are to pass the few days remaining to us in serious gambling. This deck is missing a pair of aces. No doubt some member of your crew has been having astonishing luck of late, *hein?*"

The seaman laughed and said he'd see what he could do. When they were locked in again, Gaston took his tin plate in his lap and went to work on it as he chuckled

70

fondly to himself and said, "Such innocent children you recruit for your navy, Dick. I was afraid he'd ask about a certain piece of cutlery, but, as you see, he did not!"

"Jesus H. Christ! You held back a knife and got away with it?"

"*Mais non,* anyone who's spent as much time as I in various jails knows better than to try to steal a *knife!* Knives are counted. Spoons are no doubt supposed to be. But as I handed back our mess gear, all cluttered together, as you lay in the arms of Morpheus . . ."

"Gotcha," Captain Gringo cut in. "But what the hell are we supposed to do with one lousy spoon?"

Gaston got up, moved to the door to make sure nobody was near enough to matter, and slid the stolen spoon from his shirt, saying, "There are spoons and there are *spoons,* once one knows how to work metal, *hein?*"

He hunkered down near his younger companion and showed him what he'd done to the spoon, as they both sipped coffee, heads close together. Captain Gringo whistled. The bowl of the spoon had been flattened by Gaston's boot. He'd scraped it to a spade-shaped point. A sharp one. Captain Gringo said, "You sure were a busy little bee while I was asleep."

Gaston said, modestly, "I had a loose rivet to draw it through. It's the one that's leaking so badly at the moment. I thought I'd kill two birds with one spoon, *hein?*"

"Are you nuts? Even if you could work enough rivets loose to matter, we're on the high seas, at the *waterline!*"

"True. Relax. I have no intention of carving my way through a steel hull with a kitchen spoon, Dick. I simply want to work a mouse hole here and there before we put in to Mexico."

Before Captain Gringo could ask him what he meant, the door opened again and the same seaman came in to tell them he had to take the tray and utensils back to the galley. He handed Gaston a fresh deck of playing cards before adding, "I know it's not like you guys have to eat in a hurry, but the J.G's given orders. He says I'm to count all the cutlery, too. Ain't that something?"

Gaston innocently smiled up at him, having slipped the knife-spoon out of sight, and said, "I'm sure you'll find we have not swallowed any silverware, this time. Tell me, is there any chance we could have some tobacco and matches?"

The young seaman glanced at the heavy set C.P.O in the doorway and asked, uncertainly, "Chief?"

The C.P.O. shrugged and said, "Sure. Why not? There's nothing in here anyone can set on fire."

The seaman said he'd see if he had any butts to spare. Captain Gringo smiled up at the C.P.O. and said, "We won't forget this, chief."

The burly old pro repressed a grimace and said, "Yes, you will. We're halfway there already. But what the fuck, I run this watch and I don't need snotty J.G.s telling me how to treat prisoners, see?"

The door clanged shut. Gaston sat hugging his knees as he tried not to laugh. Captain Grigno said, "Big deal. So now we have a sliver of steel, two decks of playing cards, and hopefully some smokes. What's so funny, dammit?"

"Your droll Lieutenant Carson. After plotting a Byzantine trap worthy of a Borgia, he has, how you say, fucked himself just because they never taught him never to cross your senior noncoms."

Captain Gringo shrugged and said, "Okay, so the crew doesn't like the prick. They'd have to be freaks if they did. The chief has his nose out of joint because Carson's been giving him chickenshit orders. That doesn't mean he's about to help us escape, you know."

Gaston shook his head and said, "But, Dick, he already *has!* As soon as I have matches in my hot little hands,

72

I shall proceed to show you how an old jailbird does his, how you say, stuff."

Captain Gringo stared around at the four steel walls, steel ceiling, steel deck, and said, "Right. You're going to cut through steel plate with a wooden match, huh?"

Gaston said, "I am. But you are such a stubborn willful child I don't think I'll tell you how, just yet. You really must learn a proper respect for your elders, Dick. Did you really think they could hang a brilliant criminal like me, if they gave me all these hours of privacy as well as the tools of the trade?"

Despite all Gaston's bragging, and he bragged a lot in the time left, it was still a damned near thing. The skipper pushed the old tub hard, as if he wanted to get rid of the unpleasant Carson and his prisoners as soon as possible. But as they steamed up the coast toward their slated dooms, the two prisoners worked like hell, taking turns at the door as the other used the one improvised knife to shred the two decks of playing cards.

Captain Gringo didn't think it would work. But what the hell, it passed the time. He'd never noticed, until Gaston pointed it out, that standard playing cards were made of printed pasteboard coated with celluloid. By cutting the cards up a bit and working the edge of the honed spoon between card and coating, it was possible to peel off flakes of pure celluloid.

They looked a lot like the dead skin one peeled off a bad sunburn. Gaston saved every scrap, getting rid of the leftover paper by chewing it to a pulp and spitting it into the honey bucket they'd been issued to shit in. Since nobody gave a damn about examining human shit, the waste pulp was taken out and dumped overboard regularly.

Gaston hid the celluloid by stuffing it in seams after digging out the calking with his spoon-knife. When Captain Gringo asked him how the hell he'd ever get it out again, Gaston said it didn't matter.

As an ordnance expert, Captain Gringo didn't have to wait until Gaston had used up both decks of cards and started tamping the shredded celluloid with hoarded, compressed white bread before he told his enthusiastic comrade it just wouldn't work. He said, "I know nobody but a nonsmoker should wear a beard and a celluloid collar at the same time, Gaston. But the stuff's just highly inflammable, not explosive!"

"Pooh. Guncotton is only highly inflammable, outside the gun. This latest wonder of modern chemistry will never replace hard rubber, gutta-percha, or other sensible *plastique* materials until they learn to dissolve the cellulose in something less *dramatique* than nitric acid, *non?*"

"Yeah, yeah, I once tossed a busted celluloid pocket comb into a camp fire and it poofed pretty good. But you've got that shit stuff in wet rusty steel, tamped with moist bread."

"What of it? The nitric acid is the oxidant, you species of pessimist. Here, take this blade and start unraveling my blanket. Wool yarn mixed with the bread will form an even stronger tamping, *non?*"

Captain Gringo did as he asked. At least it gave Gaston something to do. As the hour for dropping anchor off Mazatlán approached, it was getting harder and harder to avoid needlessly sentimental conversation.

He was going to miss old Gaston, for a while. They'd been through a lot together. But, what the hell, they'd both be dead in a few days. He wondered if it was true that the army hangman lashed a board to your spine to make it snap high and neat as they dropped you through the trap. He wondered if it was true that a hanged man always had a hard-on when they took him down. He didn't think he'd better discuss it with Gaston. Mexican hangmen were said to be less professional than the ones in the States.

Having finished Gaston's experiment, they had nothing left to occupy their minds and hands and were running out of dirty stories when, one morning, noon, or night, it was hard to tell, they noticed that the deck had stopped rolling under them. The vibrations of the screw died down a little later. Then they heard the distant thunder of anchor chains, and Gaston said, "We made good time. Hand me the box of matches, Dick."

"Hold it. Somebody's coming."

The door clanged open to reveal Lieutenant Carson, wearing full dress tropic whites and a self-satisfied smirk. He said, "Well, gentlemen, it won't be long now. We've put into Mazatlán and Mon-Sewer Verrier will be going ashore soon. The greasers are having some sort of fiesta. I just sent a message to the local authorities, and as soon as we can find someone sober enough to take you off our hands, you'll be on your way to your execution, Frenchy."

Gaston smiled pleasantly and said, "My regards to your mother, m'sieur. Could you tell us what time it is? Some species of insect in a sailor suit stole my watch some time ago."

Carson shrugged and said, "It's just after sundown. Don't be in such a hurry to leave us, Frenchy. I promise you we'll have you off our hands by midnight. The greasers who want you have to be *some* damned place in town. They'll probably execute you at dawn. Have you ever watched a public execution, Frenchy?"

"Oui, but I doubt I enjoyed it as much as m'sieur. I never masturbate in public places."

Carson laughed cruelly and said, "You're going to shit your pants in public, Verrier. They always shit their pants when the rope snaps tight around their neck and stretches it a foot!"

Captain Gringo muttered, "Oh, hell," and started to get up. What could they do to him for punching the ass-hole in the nose, hang him?

But then another voice from out in the companionway snapped. "That will do, lieutenant. I'll have none of that aboard my vessel."

"I was just informing the prisoners we'd arrived, captain."

The door slammed shut as their voices moved off, so they heard only the louder words as the skipper chewed out the sadistic junior officer.

Gaston struck a match as he said, "The commander's not a bad sort. I hope he does not drown." Then he lit the end of the wick he'd improvised from shredded blanket and ground-up match heads, as Captain Gringo gasped, "Wait a second! Let's *talk* about this!"

But Gaston had already balled up wet blankets and wadded them in place, and he said, "Get over here against this bulkhead with me. I don't think we'll get hit with anything at this angle, but, *merde alors,* I wish this compartment was bigger!"

Captain Gringo gulped, rolled over, and flattened out against the cold steel next to Gaston as, for a million years, nothing happened. Then, just as he said, "It's fizzled," the improvised guncotton charge detonated with a deafening roar.

The overhead Edison bulb was shattered by the shock wave, so they couldn't see what was happening. But they could feel it. The sea water rushing in knocked them both to the deck and hosed them against the far bulkhead.

Neither could make himself heard above the roar of water. So Captain Gringo could only hope that Gaston was following as he bulled his way through knee-deep swirling water, and groped blindly until, finding the jagged edges of the hole they'd blown in the side of the

76

hull, he ducked his head and hauled himself through it against the current.

He started swimming underwater, staying down as long as he could. When he absolutely had to breathe, he rose to the surface, took a deep gulp of air, and swam like hell. The next time he had to come up, he saw he was well clear of the gunboat and the water around him was black as ink. So he dog-paddled in place to consider his options. The gunboat back there was clanging its alarms, blowing its steam whistle a lot, and generally raising hell as its lights slanted ominously. He saw they were a little busy to worry about him right now, so he swung around to study the shoreline as he slowly swam that way. The seaport of Mazatlán was lit up like a Christmas tree. But it couldn't be Christmas, because they were setting off fireworks, too. A sky rocket burst over the ink-black hills rising behind the town. But everyone wasn't watching the fiesta. It wasn't every day a *Yanqui* gunboat blew up in the harbor. So, people, lots of people, seemed to be crowding down to the beach, pointing, shouting, and some of them laughing.

He heard Gaston but couldn't see him as the Frenchman sputtered and hissed, "Dick? Are you still with us?"

"Over here, you mad anarchist! Do you know what you've done? You've just sunk a U.S. gunboat, I think!"

Gaston chuckled and replied, "*Sacre* goddamn! What do you mean, you *think?* When I, Gaston, blow holes in ships, I do it right! Ah, *oui*, the lights have winked off. The water has reached the generator. Is not this fun? But enough of this chitchat, my old and rare. Where do you suggest we go now, *hein?*"

It was a good question. They sure as shit couldn't stay here dog-paddling forever. Ashore, he saw some Mexicans launching a longboat to attempt a rescue, robbery, or whatever. The American crew would be abandoning ship in their own lifeboats, too. He said, "Let's get out of here before it gets crowded. We'll swim in line with the shore till we find a less public place to beach ourselves."

That was easier said than done. Mazatlán was a good-sized harbor, the bastards had strung lights a long way along the shoreline, and they were both out of shape from their confinement. Captain Gringo was hurting but was good for maybe another mile when Gaston protested, "I'm getting a cramp. The light's not bad over there. I don't know about you, but I'm going in."

Captain Gringo didn't argue. By the time they made it to a boat ramp sloping into the water between two fishing boats, he was winded and beginning to wonder if any of this made any sense. They didn't have a centavo or a bullet between them. They didn't have one friend, but had all too many enemies, in the "stable democracy" of *el Presidente* Diaz. But they were still breathing.

They eased up the ramp, hopefully hidden in the shadows between the two fishing boats. The path ahead was lamplit but deserted. Everyone in town had run along the waterfront toward the sights and sounds of the sinking gunboat. Captain Gringo said, "Here goes," and casually walked out into the lamplight, with Gaston following. He saw a couple of men coming their way from the darkness to the south. Gaston saw them too, and slipped out the spoon-knife. Captain Gringo said, "Easy. They're just peons," as he kept walking to meet them, trying to look dry and Mexican.

The dim light and their own hurry helped. As the two Mexicans passed them, one asked Captain Gringo what was going on up the beach. He said, "Mexico just torpedoed a *Yanqui* gunboat. Pass the word."

"*Ay caramba!* Are we at war with them again?"

"It certainly looks like we are. Viva Mexico! Death to *los gringos!*"

78

Gaston added, "Remember the Alamo!" as the Mexicans broke into a run to get in on the action without looking back. Captain Gringo muttered, "Remember the Alamo? That was real cute, Gaston. Be serious, dammit! We have to get around this town and make it up into the hills before first light. Where the fuck is Mazatlán, anyway?"

"In Mexico, of course. We are roughly seven hundred miles south of the Arizona border. Even farther from Guatemala to the south."

"Oh, swell. Do you have any old pals in this part of Mexico?"

"Alas, the last time I was here, I was an officer in the Mexican army. I hope none of the locals still remember me. The reason I deserted, the last time, was because I was too idealistic a youth to carry out my orders to the letter."

"Oh boy. I was sort of hoping you'd come up with one of your rogues, Gaston. Don't you have *any* friends left in Mexico?"

"They've shot most of the decent rogues by now. I may be able to find some of the old bunch over on the east coast. The soldier-of-fortune business tends to be concentrated around the Gulf and Caribbean. Let me see, I used be married to a slightly soiled dove in Tampico. I don't think she'd still have a light in her window for me at this late date. I suppose our best bet would be Vera Cruz. *Oui*, all sorts of ships put in there, and Vera Cruz is so infested with rogues the two of us would not attract much attention among them.

"Okay, how far is Vera Cruz?"

"Perhaps eight hundred miles as the crow flies. A thousand or more the hard way."

"Let's go, then. How do you get out of here to the hills, Gaston?"

"Wait, it is all coming back to me. I told you I was once stationed here. I, ah, don't think one can get to Vera Cruz from Mazatlán on foot."

"Okay, we'll steal some horses. But let's get out in the country a ways first."

Gaston shook his head stubbornly and said, "*Mais non.* You must learn to listen to your elders, my adorable child! When I say you cannot make it out of here on foot, I of course include the feet of horses. Did you think I meant to walk a thousand miles on my *own* feet?"

Captain Gringo looked up at the sky. They'd stopped shooting rockets up at the tropic stars, but it was still dark, thank God. He said, "We gotta get out on *some* damned feet before sunrise, dammit! I'm not wearing a hat, my hair is blond, and by now the U.S. Navy has an all-points bulletin on us!"

Gaston shrugged and said, "They may have all drowned. They may think we drowned. Your gringo looks are not the problem. We can hopefully do something about that. Getting out of Mazatlán by land is the problem. It can't be done."

"What the hell are you talking about? Is Mazatlán an *island?*"

"*Oui,* in a *très* annoying way. Those dimly visible hills you seem so fond of are *très* steep, *très* barren, and *très* infested with wild Indians or even wilder bandits, where-ever there is water or shelter from the sun. To north and south alike, the mountains march out into the sea as impassable sea cliffs. Mazatlán lies in a crescent bitten into the coast of Mexico by the Pacific waves. The sea is calm tonight. But when the seas are up, one cannot get in or out of here even by boat!"

Captain Gringo turned to stare up the beach where the crowd had gathered. Some of the men had waded in to help haul a lifeboat up onto the white sand. He said, "Oh, shit. What do we do now, squat down and build sand castles till someone notices us?"

Gaston said, "Follow me. I have my bearings now. The main plaza is this way."

Captain Gringo fell in step beside him, but asked, "Do you really think this is a good time to hit the main drag, Gaston? We're both soaking wet, haven't a dime or a derringer, and they usually build the police stations near the center of town."

"*Oui*. Let's hurry Everyone will be down by the water, watching *Yanqui* gunboats sink and doubtless enjoying the spectacle. But any novelty wears off in time, *non?*"

Captain Gringo didn't answer. He grinned as he caught on. He hadn't been a rogue as long as Gaston, but he was learning, thanks to on-the-job training.

After they broke into the store and helped themselves to dry clothes of nondescript middle-class Mexican cut, along with sombreros to shade their features and hide Captain Gringo's sun-bleached hair, they felt safer on the streets of Mazatlán. Some people had started drifting back from the harbor now, but most were still over by the water. The people in charge of the music and fireworks had simply moved the fiesta onto the beach to combine excitements.

Gaston had of course broken open the till in the store they'd robbed. But he hadn't found much money. It was going to take serious money, or guns, to get them out of the odd blind corner in which some idiot in the past had seen fit to build a town. When Captain Gringo asked how the hell the people who lived here got in and out, Gaston explained that, like all islanders, they or their ancestors had arrived by boat, of course.

Gaston said, "Now that we are once more presentable, and have at least some drinking money, our best bet would be to loiter about the waterfront until we can steal a fishing goleta, *non?*"

Captain Gringo shook his head and replied, "Don't think like a navy deserter. The navy's expecting us to think like that. Are there any *rurales* stationed here?"

"*Mais non,* mounted police are rather pointless, boxed in against the sea. There are regular police, of course. Alas, a rather large force for such a small town, as I recall. Wait, don't go that way. The police we speak of have their station down that way."

"I know. I see the lights out front. Let's see how many of 'em went down to rescue the U.S. Navy, shall we?"

Gaston kept up with him, but protested, "Dick, not even Mexican police are *that* casual! They are certain to have at least a few men left to guard the premises, *non?*"

"I sure hope so. If there's nobody at the desk, it'll mean they have no prisoners in the tank."

Gaston frowned, then brightened and said, "Ah, *oui,* the more foxes the hounds must hunt, the better, *non?*"

Captain Gringo strode boldly into the police station. The sergeant seated behind the desk near the door saw they were dressed like people who had steady work, so he nodded politely and asked what they wanted.

Captain Gringo said, "Oh, are you alone, sergeant? It can wait till your watch commander gets back, I suppose."

He moved back to the door and called out to nobody at all, "Bring her back later, amigos. We need an officer to handle such a delicate matter."

The desk sergeant got up, passing Gaston as he joined Captain Gringo with a frown to ask him what the hell was going on out there. Captain Gringo didn't have to answer. As the sergeant gasped and sank to his knees, eyes and mouth both wide, the tall American grabbed the front of his tunic and manhandled him back in, growling, "Jesus, Gaston, did you have to use the knife?"

"What else would you suggest, my prick? Here, let's put him out of sight behind the desk."

As they dropped the corpse between the desk and the stucco wall, Captain Gringo slid open a drawer, took out a ring of keys, and snapped, "Cover the door. Switch off the lights if you see anyone coming."

Then, without waiting to see if Gaston obeyed, he moved to the nearest door off the main room, found the key that fit, and let himself into the arms locker. He said, "That's more like it!" as he helped himself to a pair of Colt .45 Peacemakers and the gun rigs and extra ammo bandoleers they could use as well. He strapped on his own gun rig, hooked Gaston's and the bandoleers over his free elbow, and ducked out to try another door. He didn't want anything in the broom closet. So he found the way back to the cell block, and, sure enough, a dozen-odd unhappy-looking guys were staring out of the cages at him. He nodded pleasantly, said, "School's out, *muchachos,*" and handed the key ring to the nearest wildly groping brown hand. He told the Indio to whom he gave the keys, "Let everyone out. If only to make it harder for the bastards. The arms room's open, so help yourselves. *Viva la revolución!*"

Then he turned and ran out to rejoin Gaston as, behind him, someone yelled, "What revolution?" and another yelled back, "Who cares? Get me out of here, God damn your mother's milk!"

Captain Gringo chuckled as they got outside, made it to an arcade, and slowed down to a more innocent pace. He said, "I hope I started something back there."

Gaston said, "You did, I am certain. Now what? Nobody ever looks on a flat rooftop, Dick."

"I know. Nobody but an asshole would be up there

under a tropic sun, wondering how the fuck to get back down unseen. Let's go over to the beach and see how the U.S. Navy's making out."

"Are you mad, Dick?"

"No, I call it doubling back across one's own trail. Who's going to recognize us in these outfits by flickering firelight? Put this gun rig and bandoleer on. If anybody asks, you're a vaquero just off the range, see? If the hills are full of wild Indians and bandits, the local vaqueros ought to be full of guns and ammo."

"I know what a man in a charro suit is supposed to look like, Dick. I know one stands out less in a crowd, too. But what do we do when the fiesta starts to break up?"

"What do you want, egg in your beer? You've got a gun on your hip, money in your pocket, and maybe a couple of minutes before you have to start running again. That's more than either of us could say a couple of hours ago, right?"

Drifting in to join the crowd along the beach from the shoreward side was no problem. Most of them were gazing out over the water. They weren't looking at the gunboat anymore. The gunboat had sunk. Now everyone was watching the fireworks as rockets exploded out there above the oil slick and floating debris.

Almost everyone, anyway. A group of dejected-looking guys in U.S. tropic whites were gathered around a bonfire. Some friendly Mexicans had provided blankets for the shipwrecked sailors. Most were just sitting on them. It was a warm night, even wearing wet duds. There was a line of refreshment stands set up down the beach past the crew of the sunken gunboat. Gaston wanted to walk wide to get to it. Captain Gringo told him not to be an asshole.

Why would innocent cowboys go out of their way to avoid a bunch of poor wet swabbies?

Still, it made even Captain Gringo feel a little uneasy, as he passed the group, to see Lieutenant Carson sitting on a blanket, gazing his way. Captain Gringo sincerely hoped his new hat was big enough. Carson didn't seem to notice him. So it was. Carson probably had a lot of things on his mind that evening.

Captain Gringo moved over to a taco stand and ordered a couple for himself and Gaston. The taco girl's hand felt nice as she handed him his change and murmured, *"El señor* is new in Mazatlán, no?"

He smiled down at her in the soft light and gallantly suggested, *"La señorita* no doubt knows all the single men in Mazatlán, eh?"

"Only the handsome ones, señor. I am called Felicidad."

He had to think about that. She was pretty enough, if you liked 'em a little on the plump side. Her heroic breasts were threatening to leap out at him over the low top of her frilly cotton blouse, and her big brown eyes were meeting his boldly. He said, "Felicidad is a pretty name. It suits its owner," as he handed Gaston his taco and wondered how to drop it gracefully. He didn't want to make her sore. He didn't want to fight her *hombre,* either. He knew if he asked her if she had an *hombre,* he'd have to fight the bastard for sure, if the answer was yes.

He bit into his taco. She surely couldn't expect further compliments from a man who's mouth was full. She said, "Forgive me, I mean no offense. But one can't help noticing *el Señor* is not Mexican. Were you on that boat that just sank, out there?"

He gulped, swallowed, and managed to keep his voice desperately calm, and his back to the sailors seated within earshot, as he replied, "No, my friend and I just rode down from the hills. We were prospecting for gold."

"Ah, that explains the bandoleers. Even so, you must both be very brave. It is said El Aquilar Negro haunts the mountains to the east these days. I know you did not meet him, for I see you are both still alive. But did you find much gold, señors?"

Gaston was kicking hell out of Captain Gringo's ankle as he smiled down at the flirt and said, "We didn't find any. That is why I didn't bring you any roses this evening, Felicidad."

She fluttered her lashes and said, "I will forgive you, if you will tell me how you are called."

He didn't know how many of the guys who might be listening behind him spoke Spanish. He didn't want to give his real name in any case. He said, "I am called Roberto. Roberto Duran."

"Es verdad? I took you for a gringo, Roberto."

"My mother had Anglo blood. Allow me to present my uncle, Don Pancho Garcia. Say hello to Felicidad, Tio Pancho."

Gaston kicked him savagely and told the taco girl, in his flawless Spanish, that he was enchanted to meet her. Captain Gringo knew why Gaston was kicking him, and it hurt, even with mosquito boots covering his ankles. He had no way of assuring Gaston he wasn't being dumb. He knew all too well the mess a stranger could get into trying to pick up a local girl at a Latin fiesta. Meanwhile, he had his back to that fucking Lieutenant Carson by the fire.

Carson would have shot him in the back by now had he recognized Captain Gringo's voice. Most of their conversations had been in English, even before Carson had entrapped him. He wondered how long the damned navy was just going to sit there. Didn't they have anyplace better to go? With the fire they were seated around shining at his back and the lanterns over the stands shining down from the other direction, this was not the time to turn his profile to Carson. So he kept staring down the front of Felicidad's dress, and she seemed to like it.

He'd finished his taco and was pondering his next move when they all heard a lot of noise just down the beach. He knew the sailors would be looking that way. So he muttered something about seeing her later, maybe, and drifted the other way out of the light before turning to get a better grasp on what the hell was up. You didn't have to join the crowd pressing around the two uniformed, yelling cops down that way to grasp that something awful had happened. Gaston had of course drifted into the deeper shade with him, and murmured, "So the jailbreak has been discovered and the fat is in the fire, *non?* What on earth were you flirting with that girl for? If you think you can hide out with a taco chicita, forget it! Girls down here who sell food don't sell anything else. She is a shameless flirt, but I learned long ago that girls like her only flirt for practice."

"Tell me something I don't know, Tio Pancho. That fucking Carson was within earshot and I had to stay in character. Most guys wandering around in big sombreros aren't as smart as you and me, see?"

"I'll Tio Pancho you, you idiot! Why did you say I was your uncle?"

"They're looking for a couple of old army buddies, not a young cowhand and his sweet old kinsman. Look, I'll call you shit-for-brains if it'll make you happy. But right now we'd better drift on up to dig clams or something. Look what those fucking cops are doing now!"

"*Oui,* I was afraid they were professional. Obviously, when one has a mass jailbreak, one checks identity papers. That triple-titted Diaz is a typical dictator when it comes to identity papers. In the days of Juarez, things were different. For one thing, not even the police could read.

Captain Gringo saw yet another uniformed lawman talking to Felicidad, and the pretty little bitch was looking their way! Gaston said, *"Eh bien,* we run up the beach to where it's dark and the odds more even, *non?"*

"We gotta get out of here!" said Captain Gringo, turning away. Then he sighed and said, "Oh shit!"

Gaston followed his gaze. Up the beach, more cops were herding people toward them. He said, "Okay. One chance. We head for the main crowd, like we're joining it. Then we ease around to the south side and see if they have it covered, too."

Gaston said he was sure they would. But at least they were moving.

They didn't see Carson by the fire now. But some of the U.S. seamen were still there. Felicidad had the cop leaning against her taco stand. But he was staring down the front of her dress now. If they eased through the middle . . .

They didn't make it. The cop with Felicidad turned his head as another shouted, up the beach to the north. He spotted Captain Gringo and Gaston. He waved them closer and said, "Forgive me, señors. I mean no disrespect, but I do not recognize your features and this is a national emergency. May I see some identification, *por favor?"*

It sounded reasonable enough. It seemed a shame to have to shoot such a nice friendly guy. But it was getting about that time.

Then Felicidad laughed and said, "Oh, Officer Lopez, you are so funny," and he said, "I am, Señorita Felicidad?"

"Sí, and I suspect you are showing off for me, too. Surely you know *los Señors* Duran y Garcia? Roberto, come over here and let me introduce you two. I thought Officer Lopez knew everyone in Mazatlán. But he is new on the force."

Captain Gringo and his "Tio Pancho" shook hands with the apologetic cop, who assured them he was only doing his duty. They said they understood. Captain Gringo asked Lopez what was going on and got a version of events at the police station that sounded pretty wild. Apparently one or more of the prisoners had gotten out of the cell block, knifed the sergeant on duty, and escaped to join the notorious rebel leader Captain Gringo. One unfortunate had been dumb enough to go home to his *mujer* and, when they'd picked him up there a few minutes ago, confessed in a confused way. He'd been too far back in the cell block to fill them in on all the details. But he distinctly recalled that someone had shouted something about another revolution. Lopez added that Ciudad Mexico had been warned by *telegrafo* to watch out for another advance on the capital by the terrible Captain Gringo.

Gaston said, "I have heard tales of this notorious *Yanqui*. It is enough to melt the marrow in one's bones to think of him at large, and possibly so near. But tell us, Officer Lopez, how do you know it is he leading the revolution against our beloved *Presidente* Diaz?"

The young cop pointed out across the now-empty harbor and said, "Those *Yanquis* from the ship he dynamited told us. Can you believe it? They say they had him under lock and key, to take him back to *los Estados* and hang him. Yet, he somehow managed to blow up the ship and escape! Is this not a matter of awesome wonder?"

Now it was Captain Gringo's turn to nudge Gaston's boot with his toe, as Gaston smiled sardonically and said, "I don't think it's that simple. He must have had confederates, here, to torpedo the *Yanqui* gunboat on the same night they planned the mass jailbreak, no?"

Lopez gasped and said, *"Madre mia!* I did hear some boys talking about a torpedo just now! They said two shabbily dressed strangers told them, down by the boatyards! Forgive me, señorita y señors, I must tell this to my captain!"

Gaston chuckled fondly as the young cop dashed away.

Captain Gringo could have killed him. He knew sooner or later someone was bound to ask Lopez where he'd heard this latest development. But he couldn't curse in Spanish or English in front of a lady.

He was wondering which way to head now, knowing they had maybe five minutes on the outside, when Felicidad called a couple of kids over and asked them if they'd roll her back to the market sheds if she let them eat the last of the tacos. When they agreed, she turned to Captain Gringo and said, "You'd better come with me. Both of you. Lopez is stupid, but he'll be back."

The two soldiers of fortune exchanged glances. Felicidad got between them, took each one by the arm, and said firmly, "Let's go. I can't hide you at my place. Those filthy police recorded my official address when I took out my vendor's license. But we'll be safe at my Tia Monica's. And I am sure she will like Tio Pancho!"

Tia Monica liked Gaston just fine. Felicidad's older female relative was fatter as well as older, but she had a nice smile, if a guy admired gold teeth a lot. The house wasn't near the plaza, which was just as well, when one considered all the police whistles blowing in Mazatlán right now. They didn't get a good look at the place from outside. Felicidad had led them through a maze of dark alleyways and across a churchyard full of moonlit tombstones before they climbed through a break in a wall, crossed the patio of a roofless, burned-out building, and suddenly found themselves having coffee and tostadas in a dark but cozy kitchen while Felicidad explained to her aunt that the three of them would be staying with her awhile.

Tia Monica didn't ask why. She just sat close to Gaston and purred at him until Felicidad turned to her own date, or whatever, and said, "Bring your cup along if you like. We have to have a serious discussion, Captain Gringo."

He shot Gaston a thoughtful look as he rose to follow her. In English, Gaston said, "I don't think so. She would have turned us in already if that was the plan. What are you waiting for, my blessings?"

So Captain Gringo followed Felicidad out of the room. It was dark as hell, but she seemed to know her way in the dark. She led him to a small room with a big four-poster bed. As she lit the candle, he noticed that the walls were painted purple. He wouldn't have chosen that orange bedspread if it had been up to him. The clash was even more violent when she sat on the bed to spread her electric-blue skirt on it, exposing one tawny knee as she leaned back on locked elbows and said, "Well, here we are. Take off your guns and anything else you like, Captain Gringo."

He removed his hat, jacket, and bandoleer, but kept his pants and gun rig on for the moment as he sat down beside her and said, "That's the second or third time you've called me that, dollface. What gave you the idea I'm this Captain Gringo?"

"Oh, for heaven's sake, who else could you be, Roberto? Do you want to play games, or shall we get down to business?"

He let the mistake about his name stand, but took her in his arms as he murmured, "Yeah, why don't we get out of this ridiculous semierect position?"

She laughed and said, "Wait, I don't want to talk about semierections just yet. You know what I am doing for you. The question is, what can you do for me and mine?"

"Tia Monica wants some too? I thought she had old, ah, Pancho."

He kissed her. She kissed back, giggling, before she said, "My, they must have had you locked up for a while

91

indeed. Slow down, Roberto. You know you'll be staying the night with me. More than one night, if you're a good boy. But I don't mean that kind of good boy. Oh, I like that blond hair. Are you blond all over?"

"I'm not going to tell you. There's only one way for you to find out. But, okay, let's get all the cards on the table, Felicidad. If you know who I am, they must have told you there's a price on my head. Why were you such a good sport back there at the beach?"

She shrugged and said, "I owed you that much. One of the men you let escape tonight was my cousin. By now he will have made it to the hills and El Aquilar Negro's band."

He whistled softly and said, "Can I take it this black-eagle bandit is a cousin of yours, too?"

"El Aquilar Negro is a distant kinsman, it is true, but he is not a bandit. Like me, he fights for *la revolución!*"

"Yeah? Which one? Last time I passed this way there were at least a dozen rebel factions, all killing each other off when they weren't shooting it out with *los rurales*. You know why Diaz keeps running Mexico, kitten? He's what Washington calls a 'stable government' because he's taught all the guys working for him not to shoot each other so often."

"El Aquilar Negro is different. He and his men and their *adelitas* have great discipline. They never rape. They only loot enough to get by. But enough of that. Is it true you know how to work those terrible new machine guns our government buys from abroad?"

He pressed her down on her back and began to fumble off his gun rig as he said, "I've traversed a Maxim in my time, kitten. Is that the play? Your El Aquilar Negro has some machine guns but doesn't know how to set the head spacing? A guy has to be careful when the action heats up, doll. Unless you know what you're doing, your gun can explode unexpectedly when it, ah, overheats."

He tossed the gun rig aside, and she didn't resist when he kissed her some more and got to exploring with his free hand. Everything he felt felt soft and sweet as angel-food cake. Or maybe jelly roll, he decided, as she let him get to home plate with a long slide up her inner thigh.

But as he started to check out her lubrication and head spacing, she sighed and said, "My comrades in the mountains have no machine guns at all, alas. That is why you must help us get some."

He said, "We'll talk about it later. Do you want the candle out?"

"No, *por favor,* I wish to see if you are blond all over as you put it in me, Roberto *mio!*"

That sounded fair. So they both stripped as fast as they could and fell into each other's arms, laughing like kids stealing forbidden fruit.

After they'd just gone crazy and come old-fashioned to get to know each other, Felicidad insisted on having a better look at him by candlelight. He was as curious. So he stood up, struck a muscle-man pose, then pulled her to her feet to turn around for inspection, saying, "Oh, very nice," as he saw she was a bit too dark for angel-food cake, albeit as soft and yummy. He knew she'd be fat by thirty if she didn't watch out. But meanwhile she was a lush complex of soft but not sloppy bulges connected by smoothly flowing curves. Her dark hair hung down almost to the middle of her thighs, in back. Thanks to some Indian blood, she had very little hair in the soft V between her plump tawny thighs.

He didn't want just to *look* at all that nice stuff. So he pulled her closer and, still standing, tried to put it in her again. She giggled and said, "My legs are too short, even standing on tiptoe. We'll never manage this way, *querido!*" And then she gasped, "Oh!" as he did get it back in by spreading his legs to lower his center of gravity while holding her in place with a palm cupped behind her on

93

each round buttock. She gasped, "I'll fall!" as she started grinding against him side to side in time with his thrusts. He had to lean back to keep from falling forward with her as she, in turn, arched her spine until her bounding nipples were aimed at the ceiling. She laughed and said, "You *are* blond all over. But if I come in this position I know I'll fall! My legs are already turning to jelly, Roberto *mio!*"

He moved her over to the bed, turned her around, and directed her to bend enough to brace her palms on the spread as he held her, still erect from the hips down, to enter her from behind. She moaned and leaned back into it as he parted her black hair and tawny plump buttocks to enjoy the view as he humped her, doggy-style. They exploded together and fell forward on the bed to recover their winds, with him still in her and her soft back pressed to his body as, inside, she pulsated on his shaft and crooned, "Oh, if you are half as good with a machine gun as you are with that marvelous thing in me right now, *el presidente* Diaz is doomed!"

He laughed and said, "Speaking of soldiering. I think it's time to set up new positions and fire at will." She didn't know what he was talking about until he rolled her on her back and was in her old-fashioned again, leaning most of his weight on one braced shoulder as, cocking one leg up, he settled in for slow steady thrusts that didn't have to prove anything, but just felt marvelous.

She said, "Stop for a while, Roberto. We really haven't settled anything yet."

He grinned and thrust to the roots. She laughed and said, "Oh, *that* was settled from the first time you smiled at me, you naughty! I mean we should talk. We can't talk and fornicate at the same time, can we?"

Then she said, "Oh, I see we can. Now that it is settled I am to be your *adelita* as we fight for Mexico together, we are going to need machine guns, no?"

"Don't look at me, kitten. This is the only rapidfire weapon I have handy at the moment."

"Oh, it feels better than your handy. I know you don't have your own machine gun, *querido*. The stupid government has all the heavy weapons. Is that just?"

"No, but that's life, Felicidad. That's how you start a government. You get all the heavy weapons. Nobody would ever pay taxes to a government that wasn't pointing a gun at 'em."

"We know this all too well, *querido*. The government has many rifles, cannon and machine guns stored atop Cerro de Basilio, down the coast at San Blas."

"Yeah? How far is this San Blas, Felicidad?"

"One hundred and fifty kilometers, Roberto. By sea it is not so rough as by land, but the seas are not to be sneezed at along rocky coast."

He stopped moving in her as he thought. He made her estimate a little less than a hundred Anglo-American miles. It was still too far to walk or swim. He said, "Those U.S. Navy guys will be stuck here until someone comes with another gunboat to pick 'em up. Add their shore patrol to the local cops, and stealing a boat doesn't sound like such a hot idea. How's it by land, Felicidad?"

"Impossible, unless one knows the way through the box canyons, and El Aquilar Negro has no wish to stop them. Not even *federales* dare the land route now that El Aquilar Negro has risen to lead the wild ones of the hills."

"But we're on his side, right?"

"Of course. All rebels must stick together. Who did you think I wished you to steal the machine guns for in the first place, Roberto?"

"Yeah, it would be dumb to think of going into business on our own. But, speaking of our own business, can we talk about those other guns later? I've got a full magazine again and . . ."

"Oh, yes, Roberto *mio!* Empty it into me! It makes me

so happy when you pump me full of such lovely love bullets!"

So he did, and although they didn't get very much sleep that night, they got enough, and by morning he'd agreed to lead a band of rebels into a *federale* fort and raid it for enough heavy weaponry to scare the shit out of everyone, including him. But what was a guy to do when a beautiful passionate woman was on top when she asked him to promise, say no?

Gaston thought it was a lousy idea. Gaston was like that. After breakfast the two women left the soldiers of fortune holed up in Tia Monica's house while they went out to cover, scout, and make some connections. Thus, Captain Gringo and Gaston sat alone in the kitchen as the younger man filled in the older and, he said, wiser one.

Gaston said, "Getting to San Blas, *oui*. Attacking the fort atop Cerro de Basilio, *non!* I know the place. It is a ruin, left over from Spanish colonial days. The last time I was there, the fort was half-drowned in encroaching jungle. Vines, palmetto, wild banana, wild cabbages, for all I know or care! If *los federales* have reactivated the old fort, I don't want to know about that, either!"

Captain Gringo started rolling a smoke from some loose-leaf Tia Monica had left them as he mused, "Look, you say from San Blas there's a trail leading across to the east coast where we can catch a boat out, right?"

"Oui, I know that trail. It's one the less intelligent Americans used during the California gold rush. It's terrible, it's *très* dangerous, but, *oui,* it leads to Vera Cruz."

"Okay, let's eat this apple a bite at a time. To get to Vera Cruz we have to get to San Blas. To get to San Blas, we need the help of Felicidad's rebel pals, right?"

"I said I voted *oui* on going to San Blas, Dick. It's after we *get* there that you lose me with mad plans about attacking forts filled with *soldados* and heavy weapons!"

"Look, we'll never get there without help from the local rebels. We already owe the girls for shelter and other comforts. If Felicidad can swing us safe passage through the rebel-controlled rough country to San Blas, said rebels are going to expect a payoff, and I don't have twenty pesos."

"Neither do I, Dick. But here's my plan. We agree to anything the girls and their friends ask. I will assume for the sake of the argument that Tia Monica is a girl and El Aquilar is a friend. *Mon Dieu,* you should see that tub of lard with her clothes off, and this Aquilar person sounds like the usual backwoods bandito. But, *oui,* we go along with them as far as San Blas before we cross them double, *hein?*"

Captain Gringo sealed his improvised smoke with his tongue and observed, "That's pretty shitty, Gaston. Felicidad said she could get some better sidearms and extra change for us before we even leave this place. And fat or not, her aunt took care of you, didn't she?"

Gaston shrugged and said, "The feeling was no doubt mutual. I had been locked up for a while, and she acted in bed as if nobody had been in her for at least ten years. When a man makes a woman come, he owes her no more. It is a myth that the favor is one-sided. For a man who spent four years at West Point, you certainly have a poor grasp of physics, Dick. Where does the law of gravity say that women and other bad habits should be harder to drop than they are to pick up? When we get to San Blas, we shall say we have to scout the *federale* fort atop that jungle-covered hill. Then we shall make like jolly snakes in the grass and slither on our merry way, *hein?*"

Captain Gringo lit his crude cigarillo and said, "We'll cross that one when we come to it. It's easier to act enthusiastic for a cause if you tell yourself you may just fight for it. I *got* the joke when I read *Don Quixote*. But, shit, it may be possible to raid the fucking *federale* fort."

Gaston sighed and said, "Alas, I recognize that look in your crazy eyes, my tactical genius! I too enjoy a challenge. But I just told you I have seen the old Spanish fort above San Blas. I was up there hunting iguana for my supper. The walls were still solid. Lime mortar and lava blocks, ten or twelve feet thick at the base. If *los federales* have reestablished the post, they will have cleared the second growth. So let us forget this tedious discussion of Cerro de Basilio, *hein?* There is no way anyone without field artillery and a willingness to accept heavy casualties is about to make the top of the cliff, let alone the walls. The girl said they have machine guns in the fort, *non?*"

"Of course. That's the whole point of taking the place."

"Merde alors, how? A corporal's squad could hold off a whole army from atop Cerro de Basilio *without* automatic weapons! The Spaniards did so, more than once, back when they were fighting the English privateers with such monotonous regularity!"

Captain Gringo blew a thoughtful smoke ring and said, "The troops of Imperial Spain were better than history books written by Protestants let on. Cortez took Mexico City with less than a regiment and they were no sissies. On the other hand, *el Presidente* Diaz recruits his gun waddies from the scum of Mexico. Every Mexican I've met who had a lick of sense seems to want to *fight* the sonofabitch!"

"That may be so. It is true both *federales* and *rurales* are recruited from the dregs of village society, with a few literate sadists as officers. But while government gunmen may lack finesse, Diaz buys nothing but the best when it comes to the guns that said gunmen bully the countryside with, *hein?*"

"We're talking in circles, Gaston. Yes, *federales* have

good guns. But *federale* troops are led by officers who should be locked up in lunatic asylums with their *presidente*. So, like I said, we'll see."

Gaston still would have gone on arguing, had not Tia Monica come in just then, carrying a big shopping basket and wearing a self-satisfied smile. The fat woman dumped the contents out on the table between them, saying, "Felicidad told me to get these things to you *poco tiempo. La policia* are making spot checks in the marketplace. She says she hopes the guns are as you described them."

The two soldiers of fortune blinked in pleased surprise at the two .38s in shoulder holsters lying atop the pile of peso notes and boxes of spare ammo. As Captain Gringo helped himself to a sidearm and checked the action, he asked Tia Monica where the hell all the money had come from.

She said, "El Aquilar Negro takes care of his friends and relations in town, señor. Naturally, people who do not wish to attract the attention of the thrice-accused tax collectors can't afford to spend a lot in one place, so it tends to pile up. Felicidad has been, how you say, passing the hat. Everyone is happy to know the great Captain Gringo has joined forces with El Aquilar Negro. They are most tired of the dictatorship of Diaz."

The new .38 was new only to Captain Gringo. It was an old Harrington & Richardson nickel-plated cheapo that had seen better days. The nickel plate was chipped off in places and the hard rubber grips were worn. But it was double action and when he looked down the barrel he saw someone had cleaned it from time to time over the years. The rifling was a bit worn, but the thing would still shoot reasonably straight, at close range.

As he put the shoulder rig on under his jacket and holstered the .38 after loading it, Tia Monica asked if they wanted her to cook up something for them. When they said no, she sat in Gaston's lap and started running her thick fingers through his thin gray hair. In English, Gaston said, "I should have asked for a full-course dinner. Do you want any of this, Dick? God knows there's enough to go around!"

Captain Gringo laughed and said, "It's all yours, you lucky dog. I don't think my member of the team would like it, even if I wanted to help you out, which I don't."

He looked at the watch he'd stolen the night before from the men's shop and saw the day was still young. He asked Tia Monica when they could expect Felicidad back. She said, "Not until after nightfall. Late. She is going to make for the hills during *la siesta,* when nobody is on the streets. It is a long hard journey to where she can safely meet with El Aquilar Negro. She will no doubt rest and eat supper in the rebel camp before she returns with our orders."

She kissed Gaston and added, "I will not be going with you boys. But we have the whole day to ourselves, no?"

"Dick, you have to help me! She weighs a ton and she likes to get on top!"

Captain Gringo chuckled as he stuffed half the peso notes and a couple of boxes of .38 ammo in his pockets. Then, since Gaston most obviously was not about to rise with Tia Monica in his arms and sweep her off to his castle, the younger man got up and said he'd see 'em around the campus.

He went to the room where he'd spent the night with Felicidad. It was early for a siesta. But he couldn't go anywhere until Felicidad got back, so he took off his clothes and flopped across the rumpled sheets. He couldn't lay anybody, either, until Felicidad got back. But sometimes it was a sort of pleasant novelty to sleep alone, especially when a guy needed sleep. And he knew he did. Even without Felicidad's active little body to distract him, he'd been too tightly wound from the recent excitement to relax completely. But now that he'd spent some time making sure this was a reasonably safe hideout, and now that he had a decent gun and money again, he felt a hell of a lot more relaxed. He knew there was no telling when he'd get to flop in a feather bed again once he left here. So he closed his eyes and just let go.

Like most knock-around guys who managed to stay alive long enough to be experienced at the life style it called for, Captain Gringo could sleep almost anywhere and anytime it seemed safe to do so. Professional soldiers, like sailors, tended to spread out such sleep as they had to have in short catnaps instead of snoring eight hours all at once and waking up dopey.

He knew he'd never sleep until Felicidad got back, so he didn't have to worry about setting the alarm. He knew he'd be wide awake, bored shitless, and ready to go by nightfall. That relaxed him even more, and he was out like a light in no time.

He'd slept a little more than four hours, a long rest for a knock-around guy, when he suddenly woke up to return the kisses of whoever in hell was kissing him. He hadn't covered his naked body with a sheet. The woman lying atop him was naked too, so his erection was rising to the occasion between her smooth thighs as she ground her hair apron around on his bare belly and tried to lick his tonsils with a passionate tongue indeed. The room was semidark, thanks to the shades across the narrow window. But he knew this couldn't be Felicidad. It felt more like a sea lion had beached herself atop him to mate.

He shoved her off enough to get her tongue out of his mouth as he said, "For Pete's sake, Tia Monica!"

She said, "Please do not call me your aunt, Roberto. I do not even feel *sisterly* to you, and I can feel between my thighs that you are also hot, no?"

"That's for sure. But let's think about this, Monica! What time is it?"

"About three in the afternoon. Felicidad has left for the

101

hills, and your Tio Pancho is fast asleep, so nobody will ever know. Won't you put it in me, *por favor?* I have been trying to fit myself over you, but I am too tiny."

He was too polite to laugh in her face, but he couldn't keep from grinning like an idiot, and she took his smile for agreement. So she rose on her locked elbows, her huge brown breasts still brushing his chest with their moist nipples as she wiggled her monstrous thighs farther apart and got her knees under her center of gravity, which of course was in line with her big fat ass.

He decided he was in trouble no matter what he did now. So he tried to slide a hand down between them to guide it up into her. It wouldn't work. Even with most of her considerable weight on her hands and knees, her smooth fat belly was still pressed hard to his.

He said, "We'd better let me get on top, doll."

She giggled and rolled off him, saying coyly, "I have never been called a doll before, *querido!*"

That made sense. Yet, as he rose to his own hands and knees to consider his options, he saw that, at least in dim light, old Monica looked a lot better with her clothes off than one might have expected. Like her much smaller niece, Felicidad, Tia Monica was made up of well-stuffed pillows connected by sensuous curves. Her double chin and fleshy jowls were treated kindly by gravity as she lay on her back, with the bone structure that now showed revealing that she'd once been beautiful, give or take twenty years and five times that many pounds. Her curves were a lot flatter this way, too, but she still looked like she was smuggling a pair of full-sized pillows under the brown skin of her chest. Thanks to her ample rump, there was no need of a pillow under her hips to present her yawning gates of amour to the ceiling for full inspection. He closed his eyes, gritted his teeth, and climbed aboard. He didn't like sloppy seconds, even from Gaston, and he was pretty sure the old bat would tell on him when Felicidad got back. But he knew if he rejected her this late in the game she'd probably stab him, so what the hell.

As he entered her, Tia Monica gave a pleased little gasp. He was pleasantly surprised, too. He could tell from the cool wetness deeper in her that she'd douched after screwing poor Gaston to sleep, and her cunt wasn't just whistle clean, it was little-girl tight.

But he soon found he was in no innocent child. For Tia Monica needed lots of muscle to move all that lard around, and she started bouncing him in her lap like he was a kid on a friendly adult's knee, a very friendly adult who enjoyed adultery a lot. Seeing that she seemed willing to do all the work, Captain Gringo just relaxed atop her, at a considerable angle, thanks to her big tits, and smiled down at her as she rolled her head from side to side and told him what an athletic lover he was.

He had to crane his neck down to kiss her when she said she was coming. She was well in the lead. For although any woman was more fun than the best fist, this one was right on the razor's edge between just okay and repulsive. She had an almost pretty face and a marvelous box, but she more than satisfied his curiosity about fat girls. He knew lots of guys preferred their women pleasantly plump, but when he made love to a dame he liked to get closer to her than was possible with Tia Monica. Aside from having to stretch his neck to kiss her over the mountain of breasts, he wasn't getting all he had inside her, even at this angle. Her big brown rump held back his balls, and, shove as he might, her fleshy thighs and fat lower belly cradled his pelvis so that almost an inch of his shaft was left out on the down stroke. But what the hell, this sure beat pissing, so he just stayed in the over-padded saddle and posted at a comfortable mile-eating lope.

Of course, she took his don't-give-a-damn lovemaking for passion rather than a way to kill some otherwise dull time. So it drove her even wilder and she pleaded, "All of it! Bruise my womb with your mighty tool, my *toro!*"

He said, "I can't, from this angle. Let's see, now ... oh, I know. Let's get up a minute."

He rolled out of her and got to his feet by the bed. But as he helped her rise, like a walrus from the waves, Tia Monica fluttered her lashes and asked, "Standing up, Roberto? Impossible. Please do not ask me how I know this, but take an experienced woman's word for it."

He told her the position he wanted her to get into. She gasped and said, "Oh, I couldn't! It sounds so undignified!"

He said, "It is. But every position looks sort of silly when you watch another couple making love. Come on, I learned it from a very dignified Chinese lady. They call it Walking the Duck."

Tia Monica giggled and asked if it was true what they said about Chinese women, as she turned her broad back to him, locked her knees stiffly but well apart, and bent over to clasp her own ankles with her hair spread across the floor at their feet. He steadied her with a hand on each big hip, and, as he re-entered her, with his own legs spread even farther to lower his hips even with hers, she gasped, "Oh, I can see your dangling things, and I can see it going in me, and I . . . Ay, ay, ay!"

It did fit deeper that way, and since most of her was out of sight as well, he could close his eyes, lean back his head, and let himself go as if she were as pretty as she felt, where it mattered. He came, hard, and kept going. He knew she wanted more, but getting it up again if he took it out was going to be a problem. She moaned in pleasure as their mingled juices ran out of her, down her big belly, and between her big breasts. He could tell she was climaxing from her astounding internal contractions. He wanted to come with her. But she suddenly fell off his shaft to lay quivering on the floor, delirious with passion.

So, not wanting to waste it in midair, he dropped down on her, got its questing turgid tip between the first folds he could find, and proceeded to hump like hell. As he came again, Tia Monica giggled and said, "You silly thing. You just fucked me between my titties!"

He moved experimentally and muttered, "So I did. It felt as fine as the real thing."

"Not to *me!* Let's get back on the bed and finish right."

"Okay. But first let me check the time. I don't think my, ah, uncle would mind all this, but have you and Felicidad worked out any ground rules about the men in your life, Monica?"

She sat on the bed beside him as he dug for his stolen watch, saying, "You must promise never to tell my niece. She is not a woman of the world like me. Felicidad has a very jealous nature, poor thing."

"Mum's the word, then. Let's see, it's going on four. *La siesta* is about over."

A distant male voice bellowed, in English, "Dick? Monica? *Merde alors,* where is everybody?"

Tia Monica giggled, reached for the wrap she'd draped over the foot of the bed, and whispered, "I must go to him, lest he find out how naughty we have been. You promised not to tell, eh?"

"Well, I sure wanted more, but, yeah, it's better to be discreet."

So they parted on friendly terms. She shut the door quietly after her as he rose, grinning, to take a whore bath at the washstand in the corner. He was starting to feel human again. Thanks to the timely interruption he hadn't had to prove anything, and, to his mild surprise, his teased dong was still semierect. He lay back on the bed and told it to go back to sleep. The stuffy little room was boring, now that he was alone in it again. He knew he'd awaken with a headache if he dozed off again in this airless heat, so he got up again and went to the slit window.

The sun would be low now, and the window faced east. He opened the drapes. As he'd expected, there was no glass. A slatted wooden shutter faced the street outside. But, with the hanging cloth out of the way, a little air seemed to be coming in. He heard voices outside and pressed his face to the shutter to peek out. He froze as he heard a familiar voice say, in English, "We'll cover you as you scout that next corner ahead, Moran."

He moved his eye to another slat. He could see them now. There were eight enlisted men with Carson. They had canvas leggings around the bottoms of their white bell-bottoms and carried Krag rifles at port arm, bayoneted. Captain Gringo wondered what the hell they thought they were doing. The C.P.O. with Carson's shore patrol must have wondered too. He said, "Begging the lieutenant's pardon, them Mexican cops said this part of town was dangerous, even for them. We're liable to catch a brick from one of them flat roofs all around any minute, sir!"

Carson stared after the scout he'd sent ahead as he replied, all-knowingly, "I didn't expect to find the escaped prisoners at the American consulate, chief. Walker and Verrier are professional rebels. I heard what the greaser cops said, too! They're somewhere in this native quarter, and I mean to find them if I have to search every house!"

The C.P.O looked startled and said, "Begging the lieutenant's pardon, we don't have any search warrants."

"So what? Mexico doesn't have a constitution, either. Trust me, chief. I'm an old hand in greaser land. You just have to show our little brown brothers who's boss." He called out, "See anybody up there, Moran?"

The point man called back, "Negative, sir. We seem to be getting to the edge of town. There's nothing but scrubby hills rising from behind some garden patches to the east."

But this time, Captain Gringo had of course gotten his gun. He was gripping it in a suddenly sweaty palm as he stood naked behind the shutter and heard Carson say, "Okay, we've run out of streets. So now we have to do things the hard way. Let's have a peek through that nearest window over there."

That meant the one he was peeking out! Captain Gringo rolled away and flattened out against the wall beside it, watching the zebra stripes of shadow and sky light spread across the bed and far wall until the shadows of two heads peering in through the slats chopped up the pattern. They sounded like they were in the room with him as the C.P.O said, "Nobody in there, sir. Siesta hour's over, so whoever lives here must have gone back to the marketplace or something."

Carson answered, "I have eyes, dammit. What's that draped over the chair by the bed?"

"A jacket, sir. I make it out a regular Mex jacket. Walker and the little Frog were dressed like white men when they got away, if they got away. I still ain't sure they didn't go down with the gunboat."

"They got away. I don't have to wait for those divers to get here to tell me that. The explosion was internal, and starboard, under the after turret where we were holding them."

"Yeah, but they had no explosives, sir. That ammo locker was cleaned out and repainted long before we put anybody in it."

"Okay, they had confederates waiting here. Verrier used to be a Mex officer. What do you need, a fucking diagram on a blackboard, chief? Some sonsabitching greasers got 'em out. So some sonsabitching greasers have to be *hiding* 'em! One empty room doth not a city make. Where the fuck is the door to this house?"

"Probably on the far side of the block, sir. They build 'em wall-to-wall down here. But, begging the lieutenant's pardon, we'd better not go busting down no Mex doors until we clear it with the skipper and the Mex police."

"I'll take full responsibility, chief. Don't worry. I've dealt with our little brown brothers before. Let's circle and find some entrances."

But the burly C.P.O. shook his head bullishly and said, "I've tangled with some natives in my own time, too, sir. I'm not worried about busting any rules. I got my crewmates *heads* to worry about, and it smarts to get hit with bricks and roof tiles! We're a hell of a ways from the harbor and the rest of our guys, lieutenant. If we have to fight our way back through this maze of narrow streets with everybody in the barrio mad at us, people on both sides will get hurt. So, begging the lieutenant's pardon, he ain't gonna bust down no doors unless I hear it from the skipper!"

Carson turned away from the window, bless him, as Captain Gringo heard him say in an ominously polite tone, "You're speaking to a commissioned officer, chief."

The C.P.O. said, just as formally, "I'm aware of that, sir. But if push comes to shove, I'll take my chances before the mast court-martial before I'll take a chance with the lives of my men! This is just too big a boo you've led us into, lieutenant. There's probably a dozen Mexicans watching us right now, waiting to see if we're out to start something. So we'll be heading back to the beach now, sir. If you still want to lead this patrol, I suggest you walk in front!"

Carson turned to someone Captain Gringo couldn't see through the slats and snapped, "Seaman, place this man under arrest! He just refused a direct order from an officer!"

A voice replied, "Make that two of us, then, lieutenant. I'm more scared of the chief than I am of you."

There was a round of derisive laughter. Captain Gringo bit his knuckles to keep from joining in as the pompous Carson cried out, "Very well, I'll deal with all of you once we get back to the others!"

Captain Gringo lowered the sweaty .38 and allowed himself to breathe freely again as he heard them marching away. He'd been hoping Carson would be asshole enough to stay behind. But nobody was that dumb, even in the navy, and, what the hell, he couldn't complain about the luck he'd had so far this afternoon.

El Presidente José de la Cruz Porfirio Diaz did not look or act in mixed company at all what most people expected a wild Mexican bandito to look or act like. That was one of the things that made him such a danger to his own and other decent people. *El Presidente* was a distinguished, fatherly-looking man in his middle sixties. His neatly cropped white hair and carefully kept white walrus mustache helped to give him the look of a refined Spanish grandee of the better sort. Which was just as well, since he tended to shoot people for mentioning his Indian blood on the poorer side of the family tree.

The richer side hadn't started out all that rich. Born a peon in Oaxaca back in 1830, Diaz had discovered at an early age that he was too refined to hoe corn and too nervous to be a bandit, so he had joined the army just in time to fight *los Tejanos* and other hated *Yanquis* under officers he soon came to loathe almost as much as he loathed gringos. It being safer by far to shoot a superior officer than a Texas Ranger in those days, Diaz had come out of the lost war of '48 a regimental commander. Apparently a pretty good one since *los Americanos* had never managed to wipe out his particular outfit. So when Juarez rose in the sixties and needed good soldiers, Diaz had joined Juarez, helped Juarez, and won Juarez.

After that, of course, he double-crossed Juarez in '67, lost the first round, then came back to win big after

Juarez died. He'd been *el Presidente* ever since. He liked being *el Presidente*. He meant to stay *el Presidente* and lead his dear children, the people of Mexico, if he had to kill every one of the stupid *pobrecitos*.

He wanted Washington and London to admire him, because rich friends are always handy when one has lots of poor enemies. So he kept his keen dislike of Anglo-Americans a state secret as he assured the outside world that he stood for peace, law, and order. His arguments were convincing. Few welcome guests were robbed or murdered in Mexico these days. *Los rurales* saw to that. They patrolled the highways and byways of Mexico, shooting anybody who looked the least bit suspicious. Hence, admiring American businessmen could travel from Nuevo Laredo to Ciudad Mexico without seeing one bandito, or much of anyone else. No Mexican with a lick of sense got anywhere near a paved road when *los rurales* were riding, and they always rode ahead of people approved of by their government. Executions, of course, were conducted out of sight of the main roads or the windows of the better-class hotels nice people stayed in.

That evening, as *el Presidente* was about to leave for the Austrian embassy to attend a ball given in his honor, a uniformed aide came into the presidential office to hand a telegram to the nice-looking old man behind the acre of presidential desk.

Diaz glanced at the ornate clock on the marble mantel across the room and said, "Just give me the gist of it, major. I forgot my glasses and I have little time."

The aide knew the old man couldn't read without moving his lips, so he said, "It is from Mazatlán, my *Presidente*."

"Ah? How is Project Sinaloa going these days?"

"Strangely, sir. A *Yanqui* gunboat has been sunk by a torpedo or something in Mazatlán harbor. Our people there say a U.S. Navy unit has requested permission to pursue outlaws deeper into Mexican territory."

Diaz frowned and said, "This is strange indeed! I gave orders not to blow up any *Yanqui* gunboats while I am trying to borrow money from those puffed-up swine in Washington! Tell me more about these people their navy is after. Are they Mexican? Nobody is allowed to chase Mexicans in Mexico but us, God damn the milk of Cleveland's mother!"

"I know that, my *Presidente*. But it seems the outlaws they are after are *Americanos*. One of them is, at any rate. The other seems to be a French national."

"Oh, in that case wire them permission to chase all they like. With luck, the U.S. Navy will tangle with that silly boy El Aquilar Negro and perhaps save some bullets for us. Speaking of those annoying guerrillas, is there anything new from Sinaloa in that wire?"

"No, my *Presidente*. But if it was not going according to plan, no doubt Mazatlán or San Blas would have wired, no?"

Diaz shrugged and said, "You are right, of course. El Aquilar Negro is boxed in Sinaloa and a deadly trap awaits him if he accepts the bait in Nayarit. San Blas would have informed us if any of his advance scouts had been spotted slipping across the state line."

He glanced at the clock again, got to his feet, and said, "I must go home and dress properly for the ball. I shall leave the matter out on the coast to you and the U.S. Navy for now. By the way, did they give us the names of the two outlaws Tio Sam is after?"

The aide consulted the opened telegram and said, *"Sí,* my *Presidente*. One is a Gaston Verrier. The other is named Richard Walker, alias Captain Gringo."

Diaz muttered, *"Madre de Dios!"* and moved back to sit down at his desk again as he reached for one of the phones on the green blotter. The aide stared down in confusion as the sly old dictator barked into the phone, "Connect me with army headquarters. Then stay on the line. I want to be connected with *rurale* headquarters, too!"

He looked up, saw his aide still standing there, and snapped, "Go wire the U.S. Navy. Tell them they have my blessings and they can send in the U.S. Marines if they want to, too! Don't you know who Captain Gringo is?"

"I have heard the name somewhere, my *Presidente*. Didn't he cause some trouble for us a while ago?"

"Trouble? You call that one-man tidal wave of destruction *trouble?* Go wire the *policia* in Mazatlán to put themselves at the complete disposal of the U.S. Navy and, oh yes, contact the Austrian embassy and give them my regrets. I shall not be attending their stupid ball tonight. With that maniac Captain Gringo loose in my country again, I have to stay right here until he's caught! He won't get away with it *this* time! This time I, Porfirio Diaz, am taking personal charge of the manhunt!"

The moon was high and the scrub was too low for comfort as Felicidad led Captain Gringo and Gaston out of Mazatlán that night. The girl had changed to more practical peon dress and wore crossed ammo bandoleers and a carbine across her shapely chest. She'd brought carbines for the two escapees, too. They didn't start to get heavy until the trail got steeper and the chaparral started getting higher and thicker. As they got farther from town, beyond the usual haunts of ranging herds of goats, the natural vegetation of the tropics began to replace the chaparral that custom decreed for any part of the world Hispanics settled. The slopes were getting too rugged even for charcoal burners, now. How Felicidad found her way once tree branches started blotting out the sky eluded them.

As they topped a rise with a view of the lights of Mazatlán below them to the west, Captain Gringo called a trail break. He wasn't tired yet. That was the point. He knew he and Gaston weren't legged up to par after their long confinement, and the way you kept recruits from cramping on the trail was to fall out for ten and a smoke before anyone started hurting.

They didn't light up. But as Gaston sat down beside Captain Gringo and the girl, he said, "God bless you, my son. Great minds run in the same channels, *non?*"

Felicidad bitched about stopping so close to town. Captain Gringo said, "I know we can still see the lights of Mazatlán, honey. That's the general idea. You see lights whizzing back and forth when a posse is being formed. Let's just get our second wind while we study whether we walk or run to the next ridge."

"But, Roberto, at this rate it shall take us all night to reach the stronghold of El Aquilar Negro!"

"So what? I like to scout strongholds by the dawn's early light before I walk in like a big-ass bird."

"Don't you trust my friends?"

"We have no choice. But they may not trust mysterious footsteps popping out of the bush at them in the wee small hours. Sentries on duty after three o'clock tend to be trigger-happy if they're awake at all. You're with a couple of old soldiers, kiddo. The way you get to be an old soldier is to avoid needless complications in an already complicated world. Old soldiers never run when they can walk. You cover a surprising amount of ground if you just take it easy and keep going. Guys who dash madly hither and yon are usually pooped out long before steady plodders are even tired."

Gaston nudged him and murmured, "Hold it down. I hear something!"

Captain Gringo answered, "I think I do, too. I make it someone on foot, running. Alone?"

"Oui, but bursting through the brush with no regard for the slope, as if the devil was in hot pursuit! Don't you think we've rested long enough?"

"Hold it. Let's see what he has to say for himself."

To lever the Winchester action would be noisy. The guy puffing up the trail would probably fall down just as well with pistol balls in him. So by unspoken agreement the soldiers of fortune drew their revolvers and waited, covering the trail. As a light below was blocked out by someone's bulk in front of it, Captain Gringo called out, *"Helar! Quien es?"*

Tia Monica replied, with a wheeze, "Is that really you? Thank God, I thought I would never be able to catch up with you!"

They put their sidearms away as the fat woman staggered up to them, gasping, and weakly flopped down. Felicidad asked her aunt what on earth had made her run up the trail so fast. It took Tia Monica a while to answer. Then she got her breath, enough to talk anyway, and said, "I got out the rear window. I don't know how either, but I did. They were breaking down the front door. We have been betrayed!"

Captain Gringo asked, "Who was it, a shore patrol of *Yanqui* sailors?"

"No. *La policia!* They knew right where to come! They did not knock on any other doors. That was how I knew they were on serious business."

Felicidad gasped and asked, "Who could have told them? Nobody but a few of our trusted friends knew!"

Captain Gringo grimaced and said, "Next time, be careful who you trust. That's one of the problems when you start any revolution. The government always pays better, and some sonofabitch is always greedy. Did they see you sneaking out the back, Tia Monica?"

"Would I have made it this far if they had, Roberto?"

"Right. It was a dumb question. Okay, how far are we from the rebel stronghold, Felicidad?"

"It is hard to count kilometers when the land rises and falls so. In hours, it is six or more, depending on how fast we move."

He thought, then said, "Yeah, it's too far to carry Tia Monica, and she's too bushed to go much farther. Okay, Tia Monica, here's what you do. Go back to Mazatlán and turn us in."

Even Gaston blinked at that one. Tia Monica gasped and asked, "Are you mad, Roberto? I am a woman of *la revolución!* I could never tell *la policia* anything!"

"Sure you could. Just go to the station and tell them you heard they were looking for you. That ought to get you off the hook. They'll sit you down and either offer you a cigarette or shine some lights in your face. Either way, they won't torture or even arrest you if you co-operate like hell."

"Now I know you are mad! I have never been a good liar, and I know too much! What if they forced me to tell them about you and where you are going?"

"That's the whole point, Tia Monica. They already know you girls hid us out last night, that we've left, and that we're heading for the hills to join the other rebels. If you say we forced you to hide us, and that you're mad as hell about it, they ought to believe you. The rat who turned you in has already told them pretty much the same story, see?"

Tia Monica started to cry. As Gaston comforted her, Felicidad said, "If what you say is true, Roberto, why are we just sitting here instead of running like the wind?"

"Hills are too steep. Don't worry, doll. If they had any intention of chasing us tonight, they'd have been here by now. You get to be an old policeman the same way you get to be an old soldier—by not making dumb moves.

They know we're armed and dangerous. They know we're too far ahead to chase on foot and that we'll hear horses far enough off to set up all sorts of neat ambushes in the dark. They went to Tia Monica's hoping to nail us before we left. Now that they know we have, they'll wait until dawn to come after us, if they come at all. I don't think they will."

Tia Monica asked, "What if they ask me where the stronghold of El Aquilar Negro is, Roberto?"

He said, "Tell 'em. If they have paid informants working for 'em, they already know. That's why I don't think they'll ride after us, now that they know what a lead we have. If they had the manpower and manhood to ride into El Aquilar Negro's guns, they'd have done so by now, see?"

She did. Her voice was filled with wonder as she said, "Oh, Roberto, you are so wise! Even I can see, now, that the best way to fool *la policia* can be to cooperate with them at times. How did you learn so much about fooling the authorities?"

"By *not* fooling them a lot of times. We're going to have to shove on now, Tia Monica. Get your breath. Then walk, not run, back to town. Try to make it to the police station without getting arrested on the street. Ask them if it's true there's a reward on Gaston and me. That ought to keep anyone from hitting you before they figure you're on their side. Tell 'em Gaston and me held guns on you girls and that the last you saw of us we'd kidnapped Felicidad. She may want to go back to Mazatlán someday."

Felicidad asked, "Why should I wish to go back before we win *la revolución,* Roberto?"

He sighed and said, "Trust me. I know more than you do about revolutions, kiddo."

•　•　•

As they approached the rebel stronghold by the dawn's early light, Captain Gringo felt even smarter. He knew Tia Monica never would have made it this far, and he was pretty sure nobody else was going to try without more men, more guts, and more mountain artillery than the Mazatlán police had handy.

On the map, the foothills of the Sierra Madre ran more or less in line with the coast to the west. In real life, the jagged ridges and deep canyons ran just about any way they damn well pleased. Something awful had happened to this part of Mexico a while back. Mile-thick slabs of stratified bedrock had been heaved up at crazy angles. Then volcanic crud of every description from natural cement dust to ropy black lava that still looked fresh had bubbled out of the planet's bowels to mess up the landscape further. Time and water searching for a way to the sea had eroded the already steep slopes to add a maze of jungle-choked, hairpin canyons to the confusion. The trail Felicidad knew zigzagged and roller-coastered through endless natural ambushes formed by hogbacks, buttes, castellated rim rock, and weird formations a geologist would have gone nuts trying to classify. They crossed a white-water stream, a quarter-mile below them, via a sickeningly swaying rope bridge that some optimist had built long enough ago that the yucca cables looked dangerously rotten. On the far side, Captain Gringo looked around for the guys he'd have posted here to cut the ropes when and if gray *rurale* sombreros appeared on the Mazatlán side. He didn't see any. When he asked Felicidad how come, she just shrugged and said she was an *adelita*, not a *soldado*. Gaston nodded and said, *"Merde alors,* it is as I feared. The rebel *soldados* are not *soldados*, either. Mexican revolutions are *très fatigue*, Dick. As I keep trying to tell you, Diaz hired all the real professionals, or shot them, as soon as he took over."

Captain Gringo didn't answer. Gaston wasn't telling

him anything he didn't know. He and the dapper little Frenchman had met during another rising against Diaz, not all that long ago or far away, and had as much trouble with the guys who were supposed to be on their side as they'd had with the *rurales* and *federales* on the enemy side. Meanwhile, since nobody but Felicidad had any idea where they were at present or where they were going, they had little choice but to follow. Gazing to the south across the endless sea of jagged peaks, he figured he could possibly bull through to San Blas on his own, in a year or so, given a year's supply of rations and the mules to pack them. There had to be an easier way.

Felicidad stopped on a steep slope to catch her breath as she pointed up at what looked like a thousand-foot-tall potato, stood on end and split to the ground with God's ax. She said, "Beyond that portal lies the camp of El Aquilar Negro."

Gaston said, *"Eh bien,* he is well named. Eagles usually live in high nests."

Captain Gringo didn't answer. He was looking for the lookouts he'd have posted up there where the trail followed the hog back between the natural gateway of granite. One man with a little hair on his chest and a lot of ammo for his rifle could probably stand off an army from up there. But he didn't see man, boy, or anything else living except a big turkey buzzard perched atop one fang of the natural gateway as if it were trying to tell him something. He muttered, "If there was anyone posted within rifle range of that buzzard, it wouldn't be sitting there. Rebel armies always use buzzards for target practice."

This time Gaston didn't answer. Felicidad started walking again, so they followed her. When they passed through the cleft in the rock, the buzzard was wheeling aloft at a safe distance. There wasn't even a cigarette butt to indicate anyone had ever noticed they could cover the trail to the west pretty good from up here.

When they came out the far side, they saw the camp of El Aquilar Negro spread across the valley floor beyond. It was a nice place to camp. The valley floor was flat and covered with grass. A stream of cool mountain water meandered across the natural meadow. The tents and brush shelters of the rebel "army" were strung along the banks of the winding stream. Horses and other livestock grazed about the camp freely and untended. Their owners were doubtless right in assuming the stock wouldn't stray far from good grass and water. It was still a hell of a way to run a railroad. As if he'd said so aloud, Gaston nodded and said, *"Oui,* Saint Cyr and West Point both agree that one occupies the high ground and sets up *some* sort of perimeter. At least they have a flag."

Captain Gringo didn't think much of that, either. As a vagrant puff of breeze lifted the red flag over a bigger tent, he saw that it was a red flannel bedspread on which someone had crudely painted a black Aztec eagle. He didn't ask, but Felicidad said that was where they'd find the great El Aquilar Negro. So they followed her down the slope.

Some women, children, and one guy with a rifle slung over his shoulder showed some interest as they approached the headquarters tent. Another guy in peon white cotton and a stolen army cap stood in the open entrance and, as they got within earshot, called out to ask if they had any quinine. They said they didn't. He waved them closer anyway, saying, "The general is in a bad way. It is the ague, we think."

The newcomers crowded into the tent. There were others on their feet or hunkered down inside. A rather handsome but pudgy-looking guy of about thirty lay on a cot, covered with quilts but shivering anyway. Felicidad gasped, "What has happened, El Aquilar Negro? You were all right when I spoke to you just last night!"

The rebel leader tried to sit up, gave it up as a bad move, and smiled up weakly at them as he said, "It is nothing. It will pass. Are these the professionals you told me about, Felicidad?"

The girl introduced him to Captain Gringo and Gaston. El Aquilar Negro said, "Forgive me for not offering to shake hands, señors. I do not think what I have is catching, but why take chances? You are most welcome indeed. Your fame has preceded you, and God knows we could use some professional advice! What do you think of my little army, so far, Captain Gringo?"

"You're right. You need professional advice. Fortunately, the Mazatlán authorities do too. So you guys are probably okay for now."

"It is said the U.S. Navy has come ashore to help the government search for us. *Es verdad?*"

Gaston nodded, but Captain Gringo said, "I'd better level with you, general. Those gunboat troops aren't after you. They're after us. All in all, it might be in your best interests to show us the way out of here, to the south. If we're not here, they won't come here after us. Without heavy weapons, we're no great addition to your forces."

"But you are a most famous machine-gunner, no?"

"That's what I just said. Gaston, here, can drop mortar or artillery shells in a barrel from a mile or more away. But do you have anything heavier than a saddle gun to issue anybody?"

El Aquilar Negro sighed and said, "Not yet. We were just about to raid the *federale* fort at San Blas to get lots of good things. Alas, as you see, I am not in shape to make it to the latrine on my own at the moment. But I have had this fever before. It will pass, in maybe a few days. Meanwhile, consider yourselves at home. We have plenty of food, plenty of wine, and plenty of women, if you do not already have an *adelita.*"

Felicidad put a possessive arm around Captain Gringo's waist as he said, "We've got everything but plenty of *time,* you mean, general! We know the guy who'll be leading the shore patrol ahead of God knows how many Mexican government men. We know he's a fanatic who enjoys hurting people. We know some of your so-called friends in Mazatlán are informers. So what will you bet they have this camp pinpointed on the map? The only reason they haven't hit you already is because, yeah, you and your people are forted up pretty good in these hills, and, up to now, they've overestimated your forces and were waiting for somebody to lead them."

El Aquilar Negro looked even sicker than he said he was and asked, "What can we do? This valley is too perfect to give up without a fight. I know we could hold it against the whole *federale* army if we only had a few good weapons. But I won't be able to lead the raid for them for at least a few days more!"

Captain Gringo turned to Gaston and said, "You know Mexican S.O.P., Gaston. How long do you think it will take them to probe this far?"

Gaston shrugged and said, "You said those other navy men showed common sense. The Mazatlán police will be even more hesitant. To keep from having distressing Little Big Horns in rough country, one moves into it with caution. Each natural ambush must be well scouted before the main column marches on. We passed more natural ambushes than I could count. Say at least a few hours to circle each with a diamond patrol, and hopefully they won't get close enough to worry about, for, oh, a few days."

Captain Gringo nodded in agreement and said, "We could get luckier and they could be waiting for some back-up from the *rurales* or *federales.* But we have to assume they'll make it to that big potato within seventy-two hours. San Blas is a hell of a lot farther, but legged-up guys not expecting to be ambushed on their own ground could make it there and back easy."

"*Mais non.* They could make it, just, but it would not be easy! Assume a ferocious forced march, both ways, and it still leaves no time to scout the fort atop those cliffs, let alone take it! Forts are built with the droll intention of withstanding sieges, my enthusiastic marathon runner! Do you seriously think anyone could march almost a hundred miles, through rough country, reduce a fort with a handful of guerrillas, and march back with heavy loads in seventy-two hours?"

"Of course not. It's impossible. But when the only choice is to try, you gotta try, right?"

Gaston turned to the pallid rebel leader and said soothingly, "He talks like that a lot. Pay no attention. His parents never told him the facts of life. He thinks everyone is made out of whalebone and rawhide. I, Gaston, will think of a more sensible way."

But El Aquilar Negro stared up at them thoughtfully and asked, "If I gave you the men to do it, could you do it, Captain Gringo?"

"I said I could try. It would have to be my way. Picked men, no *adelitas* slowing us down, and stragglers shot on the trail. It's a job for real *soldados,* not guys who enjoy shooting pigs and chickens and yelling *viva* a lot."

The rebel leader smiled crookedly and said, "Alas, I know all too well what you mean. I think I may have at least two dozen good men among my *pobrecitos,* Captain Gringo. But if I let you take all my real fighters, and they get here from the coast before you get back . . ."

"I'll leave Gaston here with you to secure the post, general. He was whipping Legion recruits into shape before you or I were born. If you'll give him the authority, he'll make the sons-of-bitches work for this valley whether I get back or not."

Gaston said, "Oh, *merci très bien,* you big blond sucker of cocks!"

The man on the cot said, "Agreed. You two are professionals and, as you see, I can barely sit up." He turned to one of the others in the tent and said, "Major Gomez. You have been listening. These are my orders. See that they are carried out. Captain Gringo is to lead a picked raiding party to get us the guns and ammunition we need to do this business right. Lieutenant Verrier is promoted to brevet colonel and will take command of the remaining forces until I recover."

Gomez, a husky, bully-boy type with gold teeth, scowled and asked, "May I ask why me and my men are to be placed under gringo strangers, my general?"

Captain Gringo smiled pleasantly and said, "I can answer that, general. Do I have your permission to take this silly *cabrón* on *mano a mano?*"

El Aquilar Negro didn't get a chance to answer. Gomez gasped, "Hey, can't you take a joke, Captain Gringo?"

The tall American nodded and said, "Sure, I admire a guy with a sense of humor. Let's all get out of here now, gang. The general needs his rest and we've got some moves to make, *poco tiempo!*"

Gomez led the way out. Others, more reasonable aides who'd followed the exchange fanned out to gather in the guerrillas. As they waited, Felicidad plucked Captain Gringo's sleeves and said, "I do not understand, Roberto. Why did the general call Tio Pancho by another name?"

He said, "I guess our reputation's gotten around. We fibbed to you, doll. My real name's Dick Walker and Tio Pancho is Gaston Verrier. By now you've figured out I'm American and he's French. I was hoping to leave a few red herrings across our trail, but between those navy guys and the traitors in your movement, it seems to be a waste of time."

"I think I shall still call you Roberto. Deek is a silly name. What did you mean about taking along no *adelitas*? Who ever heard of a Mexican army marching without women to carry the supplies and make nice-nice in the sleeping bags at night?"

"Nobody. That's how come I hope to outmarch the other side a lot. We'll talk about it later, when and if. The guys are starting to line up."

The guerrilla band was, but they lined up sloppy as hell. Gomez must have wanted to keep his gold teeth. He sounded enthusiastic as hell about the idea, now that it had been properly explained to him. Captain Gringo let Gomez fill them in until he was repeating himself, then held up a hand for silence and called out, "All right, *muchachos*. The sun's up and it's getting late for any further bullshit. You know the score. I'm marching south to San Blas. Double-time on the downhill slopes and quick-march going up. We'll travel light. You can piss or smoke when I give you a trail break every other hour. Don't bring food or water. They both weigh you down. We'll drink when we cross a stream. Seventy-two hours without food or sleep won't kill anyone but a sissy. I want two squads. That's sixteen men and two noncoms. Step forward if you're tired of living. I ain't got all day!"

Almost all of them stepped forward a pace, though some looked worried about it. He picked two guys wearing stripes on their cotton sleeves and concerned expressions on their faces. He said, "You and you. I can't stand noncoms who look confident. Let's hear some names here, dammit!"

One said he was called Morales and the other answered to Robles. Captain Gringo said that was good enough and added, "You know these men. They all look brave to me. Pick out your own squads. Make sure everyone has good shoes or tough feet. I'm going to be mad as hell at you if any of them don't know how to shoot straight and carry out orders to the letter."

They saluted awkwardly and turned to choose the men they'd be leading as he heard someone mutter, *"Madre de Dios,* he's a nasty one, no?" But an older *soldado* laughed and said, "I'm going with him, if they pick me or not. It's the tough ones who bring you back alive, see?"

Robles did pick the old soldier. So, not waiting any longer, Captain Gringo said, "Follow me!" and started walking south, not looking back. As the two squads followed Captain Gringo, Gaston stared fondly at the much larger group left and said, in a parade ground voice. *"Eh bein,* my children. I see what my good fortune has left me. I assure you I feel no better about it than you scum do."

There was a low, angry murmur from the assembled guerrillas. Gaston snapped, "You are at ease, God damn your eyes! When I want you to speak I will order you to. When I want you to roll over, I will order you to. At the moment, you are supposed to be at ease. That means you keep your moronic mouths closed while I tell you all a touching story."

They subsided into sullen silence. Gaston nodded and said, "Once upon a time, when I was just a little boy, I was given a box of tin *soldados* for Christmas. I loved my little tin *soldados.* I used to line them up neatly and tell them how much I loved them. All but one, who refused to stand straight and had to be thrown in the stove to melt, *hein?* Alas, we had to move, and somehow my little tin toys got lost along the way. I was *trés* heartbroken! I cried and I cried for my tin *soldados,* but they were gone, it seemed, forever. My grandmother, a wise old woman who sold violets and picked pockets by La Opera, took me in her arms and consoled me. She said not to worry. Someday, she assured me, I would get my dear tin *soldados* back."

Gaston rocked back on his heels as he gazed at them fondly and added, "My grandmother was right. Today I have my tin *soldados* back! Your paint has rubbed off and I see none of you can stand straight now. But, by my grandmother's bones, I have you little tin bastards back at last, and I mean to have you looking and acting like *soldados* again! We shall begin by coming to attention. I said, *attention!* Right dress and cover down! Move it, you species of triple-titted toads!"

Some of them tried. Others just stood there, gaping. One made the mistake of laughing out loud. Gaston walked over to him, asked, "Is something funny?" and kicked him in the balls.

As the guerrilla dropped at his feet, moaning in agony, two of his buddies surged forward, then stopped, as they saw they were staring down the muzzle of Gaston's .38. Gaston smiled pleasantly and said, "Do not try it, *muchachos*. I am not attempting to win any popularity contests here. We have less time than we need to shape up and secure this stronghold. I can't use men who argue with me. So do yourselves a favor. Don't argue!"

They got back in line, at attention. Now that they saw Gaston wasn't kidding, the others tried harder to form a straight line. He nodded and said, "You still look like the snaggle teeth of a badly beaten whore. But that's better."

Major Gomez had been watching all this, of course. He came over to Gaston and said, "Hey, why are you picking on my boys, Frenchman?"

Gaston shot him.

The lined-up guerrillas gasped collectively as their major sank to his knees with a startled expression, then flopped forward to lie dead at Gaston's feet. Gaston said, *"Eh bien.* As I was saying, we do not have time to argue among ourselves. You have my permission to hate me, you poor stupid children. But the childish game of playing rebels and *rurales* is over. The real thing is marching on us as we attempt at least to stand at attention. You, you, you, take this carrion somewhere and bury it. The rest of you follow me. We are going out across the meadow for some close-order drill. I intend to shoot every mother's son who fails to leap when I shout Froggy! Then, with what is left of you sorry sons-of-bitches, I intend to set up defenses that one hopes the other bastards shall not be able to overrun with one lousy charge, *hein?*"

Since he'd started with a much smaller bunch of picked men, Captain Gringo didn't have to shoot anyone with him the first day on the trail. He had to kick a couple to their feet after trail breaks as the day wore on, but that was only to be expected and they took it in good humor for the most part.

His men were well legged up from raiding the lowlands and cutting off occasional travelers unwise enough to attempt the mountain trails without military escorts. But they were also used to knocking off every afternoon for *la siesta* and protested, as the sun rose to the zenith, that he was going to kill them all. He admitted they had a point. Their big sombreros didn't help much as the noonday sun blasted down at them at well over a hundred degrees in the shade, if there'd been much shade. He announced, "I'm about to drop, too. But look at it this way. Would you rather die of sunstroke or with hot lead in your guts? We can walk faster and not screw around with scouting when not even a lizard would be dumb enough to move in these hills. *Los rurales* aren't as tough as you guys. So they'll be holed up somewhere with a cerveza, a *puta,* or both."

Someone croaked, "Let them keep the whore. Just give me the beer!"

Captain Gringo laughed and said, "You never had it so good. We're topping the rise. So ... double-time, march!"

Behind him, as he jogged down the slope under the tropic sun, he heard someone gasp, "He's inhuman! I can't run another step!" But Corporal Robles snapped. "You will run as far as he says, or I will kill you. I picked you for a man, *niño!* Are you going to make a fool of me? No, by the beard of Christ, you are *not* going to make a fool of me! If you let me down, I shall leave you by the trail with both kneecaps blown off. Then, when we get back to camp, I will ravage your *adelita* cruelly before I shoot her, and your children, too!"

That seemed to work. When Captain Gringo called quick-march up the next slope, all his guys were still with him.

He drove himself, and them, until the sun was lower and a more reasonable shade of orange. He halted the column near the top of a ridge to the south and told them to fall out. They did so, literally. A couple just flopped on the trail as if they'd been shot. He didn't want them getting shot. So he called out, "Morales, bring the map and follow me." Then he eased up the trail a way, stepped off it, and dropped to crawl the rest of the way over the rise through the brush. He stopped with his outline hopefully broken by the chaparral all around and was staring down across the valley to the south where Morales joined him to ask what was up.

Captain Gringo said, "Anyone could be up, now that *la siesta* is over and this chaparral is down. Look at the bushes around us. Goats have been grazing this ridge."

Morales said, "*Sí,* but we know the people who ranch down below. They are simpatico to our cause, Captain Gringo."

The American spotted the outlines of a ranch house, almost hidden by the trees around it. He asked. "How simpatico?" Are they fellow rebels or just people who don't like the current government all that much?"

Morales shrugged and said, "Nobody likes the current government, Captain Gringo. They allow us to water our horses there and they never turn us in to *los rurales*. In return, we never raid them."

"I get the picture. Let's see that map now. If we're still on El Aquilar Negro's hunting grounds, we're not far enough south to matter. We'll have to make up the lost time by pushing harder in the cool of night."

Madre de Dios, Captain Gringo, you expect us to march *faster?*"

The American spread the map and found their position. He swore under his breath and said, "I know it's impossible. We have to do it anyway. We're not even halfway to the border between Estados Sinaloa and Nayarit yet, dammit!"

"I know. My feet are killing me. Forgive me. I mean no disrespect, but I know my men, and their feet are killing them, too. We have bullied an amazing march out of them. Perhaps they can walk almost as far once it cools off, as you say. But they must have some rest before pushing on. Food would not hurt them, either. The rancheros down there have food. They are far from any *rurale* post. God knows when we shall encounter such good fortune again, Captain Gringo. I do not know the country beyond the next spur running west to the sea."

Captain Gringo muttered, "That makes two of us," as he studied the map. There wasn't much to study. The guerrillas had lifted it from an unfortunate traveler who'd used it to get lost in their part of the hills a while back. It was a standard Mexican ordinance map, with gross features probably about where they should be. There was a hell of a lot of blank paper between inked-in roads and towns. Neither this ridge nor the ranch in the valley below were on it. The bright side was that the enemy might not know the country any better. He said, "Well, we're still close to seventy miles from San Blas. We'll have to slow down even more and put out point and flank scouts once we get closer. Okay, run down there and ask 'em if they want a fight or extra dinner guests. If they don't kill you, I'll bring the others down when you signal." As the man turned to go, he added, "Oh, yeah, Morales?"

...."*Sí*, señor?"

"If I see you just waving, I'll know they have the drop on you. So I'll rescue you if I can, and if I can't, tough shit. If it's really all clear, signal me by hopping on one leg. That's about the last thing I can think of them forcing you to do."

Morales chuckled and said he understood. Captain Gringo watched with approval as Morales crabbed sideways through the brush a hundred yards before rising to approach the ranch below from another angle through the waist-high chaparral. He nodded and silently said, "Good thinking. Don't get killed if you can help it. Good noncoms are hard to find these days."

Morales looked pretty silly hopping around on one foot. The vaqueros of the rancho were still grinning about it when Captain Gringo led the others down the slope. They crossed a wagon trace running east and west. Captain Gringo raised an eyebrow when he saw the rubber-tire tracks edged sharply by the setting sun. He kept his thoughts to himself. Damned few people could afford the new horseless carriages back in the States. They cost even more down here. While waiting up on the rise with Robles, Robles had filled him in more on this spread. Apparently there was a lot more money in raising beef and goats than he'd thought.

As the half-dozen vaqueros escorted Captain Gringo

and his men over to the main house, a woman in black widow's weeds was standing on the veranda. This didn't surprise him. Robles had said the valley was held by the widow Perez. But Robles hadn't told him what she looked like. So he was surprised to find the dame was gorgeous.

As he approached, doffing his sombrero, she said, "I am called Pilar and of course my house is your house. But thank God you did not arrive less than an hour ago! You just missed *los rurales,* or, to be more accurate, perhaps they just missed you! You caballeros are of El Aquilar Negro's band, no?"

He studied her words, and her, before answering. Pilar Perez was about thirty. Tall for a Mestiza, albeit shorter than most American girls. He figured she was maybe three-quarters white and one-quarter very pretty Indian. Her face was dusky rose in the sunset light. Her eyes were big, black, and slightly slanted by her high cheekbones. Her hair was parted in the middle and hung down to her shoulders, shiny and black as raven's wings. She was built like a well-known brick edifice and he could tell it was all her under that thin black dress. She hourglassed naturally, without the corset most women would have needed for a waistline like that between such heroic upper and lower halves of her torso.

He said, "We may know El Aquilar Negro, señora. Tell us more about *los rurales.*"

"They were just here, in an armored motorcar. They drove in from San Blas, they said, to make sure nobody was here but us and my livestock. We were very frightened. But, come, they are gone for the night, I am sure. They said they were patrolling back toward San Blas, along the coast road. You and your men must be hungry after such a long journey over the rim rocks."

That was for sure. But Captain Gringo turned to Robles and said, "You and your squad stay out here and set up a perimeter. When Morales and his men have eaten, they'll relieve you. Post your guys under the trees and make sure they don't smoke after dark. Any questions?"

"No, Captain Gringo. I am an old night fighter."

The tall American nodded, motioned to Morales, and told the woman he'd pay for some tortillas and beans for his men. She sniffed and told him not to insult her. So they all went inside.

A couple of vaqueros followed, but the widow turned to one who seemed to be her ramrod and said, "Tico, with *rurales* in these parts, you and the *muchachos* had better round up the stock. Especially the horses, no?"

The ramrod nodded and led his segundo out to attend to it. The woman ushered them back to the large combined kitchen and dining room, where two older peon women were already preparing food on the hearth of a beehive fireplace in a corner, and another woman, younger and better dressed, sat at a big plank table, nursing a mug of coffee and a sullen expression. Pilar said, "This is my little sister, Carmencita."

Captain Gringo nodded pleasantly to her. Carmencita didn't even look at him, so he said, "Up yours," in English, and took the seat the older and better-mannered sister indicated. Morales of course rated another chair. The men with him knew their places in polite Hispanic society and squatted against the walls to be fed, if and when.

Pilar took her place at the head of the table as Captain Gringo studied Carmencita and tried to figure out what was eating her. She was a pretty little thing, whiter-looking than her older sister, with just a hint of Indian in her cheekbones and straight black hair. She, too, wore black. Her figure was more willowy, but she was a long way from being flat-chested.

Pilar caught the thoughtful look in Captain Gringo's eye and nodded to say, "*Sí*, she is a little snip. She's not angry with you. She's angry with me. I have refused to receive a certain young officer who keeps arriving with flowers, books, and candy."

The younger girl flushed crimson and started to say, or spit, something. Then she lowered her eyes to her coffee cup and murmured whatever it was under her breath. Pilar said, "Don't pout in front of company, you silly child. I agree he's very pretty, but no woman of this house will ever keep company with a *rurale* as I draw breath!"

Captain Gringo was embarrassed for them both, and wasn't interested in family quarrels in the first place. So he said, "Your government seem to be pretty busy around here lately."

She said, "Mexico has had no government since Juarez died. We do not consider that bandito, Diaz, a government."

"Yeah, but he's got a rural *gendarmerie* and a federal army just the same. You told us about *los rurales* patrolling the roads in an armored motorcar, señora. What can you tell us about *los federales?*"

Before she could answer, her chicas started putting cups of coffee and bowls of food in front of everyone who rated a seat at the table. Their hostess said, "Please call me Pilar. I only insist on señora from those others. *Los rurales* are always with us. My late husband taught me how to deal with them. By politely asking the local *rurale* commander if he would be kind enough to forward your land tax, paid in cash, one tames the beasts at little extra cost. The *soldados* who've just moved into the area are another matter. They have yet to approach me, so I don't know how big a bribe it will take to keep my livestock and the virtue of my sister and me. They are stationed to the south, between here and San Blas. We do not know just where, but they are said to be patrolling the hills between the two routes south."

Captain Gringo took out the map, spread it between her bowl and his, and said, "I have the roads. That's about all. The surveyors who drew this map must not have known how to draw mountains or canyons. Could you fill in some of the blank space for us, ah, Pilar?"

She turned and asked one of her servants to fetch her a pencil. Then she turned back to him and said, "I can try. By the way, I forget how you are called, señor."

"I am called Dick. That's Anglo for Ricardo."

"I prefer Ricardo. Deek sounds undignified."

The chica handed her a pencil stub and Pilar started marking up the map as she said, "This coast road ends at Rosario, to the north. They say someday they mean to extend it up the coast to Mazatlán, but sea cliffs still block the way. To the south, the coast road runs all the way to San Blas and the western terminus of the new railroad."

"There's a railroad depot in San Blas? That explains a lot!"

"Ah, you heard of the new ordnance depot atop Cerro de Basilio? I was wondering why El Aquilar Negro sent you this far south. Unless you and your men are just an advance patrol, you don't have the strength to take the fort."

"Is that where *los federales* are, Pilar?"

She shook her head and said, "Not all of them. Others have been seen much closer!"

She ran the pencil along the mapped inland trail and went on, "This is the logical way people who do not wish to be bothered by *rurales* in armored motorcars on the coast road would naturally take. You can reach it by traveling west, up this valley, to where the trail crosses it. I don't think I would do that if I were you. Nobody has come up the inland trail from the south for at least a week."

"Right. Armored patrol on the low road, cavalry troopers on the high road, and nobody gets to Scotland either way, right?"

She looked confused but didn't ask what he meant. She

was drawing another line. She said, "I cannot do this in detail from memory. I have only ridden a few kilometers of it in any case. But here, midway between the better-known routes south, a goat path follows the ridges south. It is difficult, even on foot. Nobody remembers who laid it out originally. Perhaps the Indians, in the old days. I shall not try to draw in all the curves and passes. My goatherds tell me once you are on it, it is not impossible to follow. The tricky part is that in places it doubles back on itself to avoid running over thin air. The hills are badly cut up by canyons. A stranger in these parts would think the old Indio trail led nowhere. That is why I don't think you would be as liable to meet anyone on it."

"I hope you're right. Where does it end, to the south, Pilar?"

"Nowhere, officially. Actually, after crossing the Rio Grande Santiago, it comes to a railroad cut east of San Blas and keep going, God knows where, to the south. When the government surveyors layed out the new railroad, they apparently didn't even notice the narrow path along the crest of a ridge they had to cut through. I have never followed the old forgotten trail all the way, of course, so I cannot tell you exactly how far it leaves you from San Blas at the south end. It is said *los federales* patrol the tracks with cannon and machine guns mounted on armored flatcars. On the other hand, the jungle is quite thick in the lowlands near San Blas."

He nodded, took back the map, and folded it, and put it away as he said, "You've been a great help, Pilar. Now I'd better finish up and let you feed the next shift so we can be on our way by moonrise."

She gasped and said, "Oh, no! You can't take the old Indian trail at night, Ricardo! Did you not hear me when I said it was most treacherous? You must wait until morning. Until just before dawn, at least. It is hard to find even by daylight. Walking it in the dark is suicidal! In

135

some places it winds along the edges of sheer drops. The vegetation grows thicker as one goes south. Some parts lead through tall timber, to hairpin on the edges of tall cliffs!"

He nodded politely as he went on stuffing his gut with refritos and coffee. The coffee would help him and the others, some. He noticed that neither of the women were eating. He'd thought they'd arrived past suppertime. Pilar watched with polite concern as he grubbed. Young Carmencita was chain drinking coffee and trying not to squirm in her seat. He repressed the impulse to tell her she was never going to get to sleep tonight if she added caffeine to the other ants she obviously had in her pants. Her problem wasn't his. It was all hers, and it seemd to be driving her nuts.

He excused himself from the table and went out to relieve Morales after telling the guys with him to hurry it up. Outside, Robles told him all the vaqueros had ridden off someplace in a hurry. Captain Gringo said, "Roundup time, she says," as he stared west at the sunset. Others who'd eaten first, with him, came drifting out as he filled Robles in on his conversation with Pilar. Robles said it made sense. He'd heard of the old forgotten trail, though he'd never traveled it. He said, *"Federale* troopers on horseback would not be able to move any faster than men on foot along such a treacherous route, even if they knew about it. I doubt if they could, since they are new in these parts."

Morales came out, belching contentedly, and said *la señora* wished to speak to Captain Gringo again. The tall American said, "Take over here. How far does that wagon trace run down the valley before it meets the main coast road? Do you know?"

"*Sí*, it is about ten kilometers, Captain Gringo. Why? Surely you do not mean to lead us *that* way! The woman says *los rurales* are patrolling it in armored motorcars!"

"Yeah, I can still see the tracks. Come on, Robles. Time to feed your squad and see what the lady wants."

Inside, neither sister was seated at the table. One of the chicas led Captain Gringo to another wing of the house, knocked on a stout oak door, and ushered him inside. Pilar was seated on the edge of her bed. She was fully dressed, but he was still surprised. Hispanic ladies just didn't receive gentlemen in their bedrooms, even chaperoned, and the chica closed the door after her as she left.

Pilar patted the bedspread beside her and said, "Sit down, Ricardo. We must talk. I know how you men are in front of others. You are afraid your men will think less of you if you show any signs of being afraid of the dark, no?"

He sat down beside her, placing his hands politely on his own knees as he replied, "I don't worry much what other men think of me. I'm not afraid of the dark, either. Old soldiers know how hard it is to snipe at anyone from ambush in the dark. I've made night marches through places you'd think I was bragging about, Pilar. Don't worry about us. I hardly ever lead a column off a cliff. Not under a full moon, anyway."

She sighed and said, "All right, let us say I am worried about us. My sister and me. Say you will stay at least until my vaqueros return, no?"

"What's up? Are you afraid Carmencita's *rurale* admirer will come calling again by moonlight?"

"Him I can handle. It is his friends I am afraid of! The ones in the armored motorcar were unknown to me. They had been drinking. A drunken *rurale*, an armored motorcar, and a machine gun are a frightening combination, Ricardo! They were very insolent, even with my men here. Ift they should return, to find us alone . . ."

"Yeah, that could be a problem. You say they have a machine gun?"

"*Si,* mounted in a little cheesebox turret atop the motor-car. I am not afraid of being machine-gunned, however. One of them was more specific about what he would like to do to my little sister."

The windows were shuttered against the night, but he could see through a slit that the sun was almost gone for good. That left twelve hours of darkness, and that wasn't enough. He asked, "How soon should your ranch hands return, Pilar?"

She shrugged and said, "*Quien sabe?* Perhaps a few short hours. I told them not to worry about the goats grazing the hills around. Just so they drive in all the horses and my prize breeding stock. Say you will keep me company until then, at least."

He sighed and said, "I'd like to, Pilar. I don't see how I can. My men and I are already trail sore. If I let them relax after a warm meal, God knows when I'll ever get them on their feet again. I figure a twelve-hour forced march ought to get us through the *federale* lines by dawn and . . ."

"You are not thinking. You are too tired to think straight," she cut in, placing a hand high on his thigh as she continued, "If you leave now, and don't fall off a cliff in the dark, you will make San Blas by day. And then what will you do? You cannot attack the fort atop Cerro de Basilio in broad daylight. You will only have to hide in the bushes all day, you silly boy! On the other hand, if you spent the night with *me,* left at dawn, and got to San Blas after dark tomorrow evening . . ."

Her hand was even higher now. He moved it away from his fly and said, "God knows that's a tempting offer, honey. It makes a lot of sense, too. But, meanwhile, my men out there are within easy reach of a motorized machine-gun crew, and you just said they may be back! I don't have a machine gun, Pilar. So, thanks, but no thanks. My *muchachos* will be a lot safer up in the hills tonight than they would be here. I don't think those *rurales* will try anything serious with you girls. They'd have done so by now if they didn't know Carmencita has one of their officers sweet on her."

He rose to his feet as she pleaded, "Wait!" and then, having run out of sensible arguments, proceeded to use womankind's oldest and most convincing one. He stood dumbfounded as she rose, too, and proceeded to take off her clothes.

He said, "You sure must want me to stay, doll!" as she unfastened her bodice and drew the black dress off over her head. His breath caught in his throat as he saw she'd been wearing nothing under it. The candlelight molded her voluptuous nude flesh in high relief and glistened on the tips of her pubic hairs as she cast the dress aside, put her hands on her naked hips, and brazenly smiled up at him as she asked, "Well, do you still want to leave?"

He grinned down at her, said, "Not really," then coldcocked her with a hard left hook to the jaw!

Pilar's head flew back, and the rest of her followed to land spreadeagled across the bed, out like a light, of course. He sighed and added, "That hurt me more than it did you, doll."

He half-turned away, had another look at the inviting way her pink slit was gaping between her widespread thighs, then grunted, "Forget it. A guy's got to draw the line *somewhere!*"

He cracked open the door, saw that nobody was outside, and moved along the hall until he saw light under another door. He opened it without knocking. Carmencita was on another bed, fully dressed, bound hand and foot with a gag in her mouth. He moved over to her, sat on the edge, and removed the gag as he said, "Don't scream. I'll have you out of these other ropes in a minute, Señora Perez."

She looked up at him like a condemned criminal who'd

just been granted a stay of execution as she whispered, "How did you know? Carmencita said she'd kill me if I breathed a word to you!"

"I noticed she talked more than she should have. If she's really Carmencita, you're really Pilar, right?"

"Of course. Oh, get my feet, *por favor!* Where is Carmencita? She has a gun under her dress!"

"Not anymore. I'll explain it along the way. We've all got to get out of here before those *rurales* she sent her so-called vaqueros for get here with that armored car!"

He finished untying her, pulled her to her feet with one hand, and drew his .38 with the other before leading her back to the kitchen. As they entered, his men looked startled and the two chicas looked terrified. He said, "Robles, tie up those two police informers and hide them someplace. Don't let anyone rape them. We haven't time. Oh, yeah, you there, run down the hall and tie up the naked lady you'll find in one of the rooms. Don't rape her, either. She doesn't deserve it."

His men were still confused but moved to obey him as he led the real Pilar outside and called in Morales and his squad. He said, "I'll explain later. I want you, you, and you to go back to the work sheds and find some picks and shovels. Move it!"

Then, as they started running, he turned back to Morales and the still-confused young widow and explained, "Nobody rounds up horses grazing in the dark, then puts them neatly in a corral, when one's worried about *rurales* stealing stock. The real vaqueros have all been arrested, along with the household servants, right, Pilar?"

"Of course. They kept me here in case anyone who knew me came by. Since you were strangers, she took my place to do the talking and . . ."

"Hey, let's not waste time on things I *know*, honey! That goat path she drew for us is a blind alley, right?"

"Yes, it only goes to a charcoal burner's camp, in a

box canyon. I know it well, since I ride my own range when *ladróns* do not have me tied up!"

"Gotcha. She was a sweet kid. Just in case she couldn't hold us till machine-gun-toting *rurales* got here, she meant to send us into a corner for them!"

The men with the shovels got back. At the same time, Robles and his squad came out of the house. Robles said, "The women are all securely bound. I am sorry, one of the boys did something bad to the one you left on the bed. I thought I'd better tell you before I shot him."

"Did she wake up while he was raping her? No? Okay, forget it, for now. But tell him if he disobeys another order, I'll shoot him myself."

He raised his voice and called out, "All right, *muchachos!* Follow me! We've got some ground to cover and some ground to dig. So pick 'em up and lay 'em down!"

He was glad to see that Pilar was able to keep up with no trouble. The young widow had horsewoman's hips and seemed used to hard, healthy living. As she trotted at his side, she giggled and said, "I am glad they raped her. But is this not bad for discipline, Ricardo?"

"Yeah, but what can I tell you? Some guys don't have as much character as me, and she sure looked tempting in that position."

Captain Gringo and Pilar sat together on a boulder as his men worked. The red laterite soil was almost as hard as brick, so they had time to tell each other condensed life stories. Her tale was shorter than his. Both of them had been in trouble for a long time. Pilar had been born and raised on the high, dry central mesas of Mexico. She'd married a nice young vaquero who'd heard rangeland was cheaper down on the rugged west coast. He'd been right about that. He'd learned why not many people tried to raise beef in the tropic lowlands when his longhorns died of rinderpest and he died of *vomito negro*.

Pilar, and a very few cows and horses and a lot of goats, was made of sterner stuff and had acclimatized to the hotter and wetter range after being sick a lot at first. She said the fake Pilar had told him the truth when she'd explained how small-holders managed to hold *los rurales* at bay by paying their land tax directly to them in cash. It had been the older and meaner woman who had the boyfriend riding for *los rurales,* and she hadn't been sending him away at all. The real Pilar frowned in the moonlight and said, "Yet, she told the truth at least half the time. I do not understand this, Ricardo. She did not have to tell you *los rurales* had been by with an armored motorcar just before you arrived, did she?"

He said, "Sure she did. The tire tracks were in the dust out front. Like all good liars, she larded her lies with truth to confuse the issue."

"I was so furious when she said it was I, not she, who admired *los rurales.* What will happen to her and those other women now, Ricardo?"

He shrugged and said, "They'll work loose or they won't work loose. They may be found before they die of thirst or they may not. Never mind about them. What about you? Do you have people you can go back to, up in the high country, Pilar?"

"Of course. My parents love me. But my father's rancho is far away. How am I to get there? I owned nothing but this range, a few animals, a *casa* with a roof that leaked in the rainy season. Now I have nothing but the clothes I wear, and . . . my body."

"Don't knock 'em. It's a pretty dress and you have a nice figure. I'd say you need a railroad ticket and enough eating money to get home to your people. We'll work it out later. Right now, no offense, I've got other things on my mind."

He stood up and called out to Morales, "That's enough. Cover the hole as I told you and then take cover." He turned and yelled to Robles, "I can see patches of white cotton in the moonlight, dammit! Get your damn squad farther back in the bushes! Haven't you guys ever ambushed anyone before?"

There were curses and the sound of dry chaparral scraping on men and metal until he called out, "That's better. Hold those positions, and remember, nobody fires till I give the command!"

Morales and his work crew finished on the moonlit wagon trace and faded back into the brush as well. Captain Gringo led Pilar behind the boulder they'd been seated on and said, "Sit down here and stay put. Don't peek over the top when the egg hits the fan. It can ruin a girl's complexion to take lead and granite dust at high velocity."

She did as she was told, but asked, "How long do you think we have to wait, Ricardo?"

He said, "God knows. A soldier spends most of his time either hurrying up or waiting. Sit tight. I have some inspecting to do."

He moved away from her through the waist-high chaparral, checking each man's position and having to move only a few to better positions. The guerrillas were no *soldados,* but at least they were experienced banditos and the plan was simple. He'd just finished and gotten back to Pilar and the rock overlooking the trap when, in the distance, he heard the tinny popping of an internal combustion engine. He drew his gun and told the girl, "Here she comes. Keep your pretty head down."

The improvised armored motorcar was a German Benz horseless carriage with a two-lung rear-mounted engine that hadn't been designed to push a mess of boiler plate, and so complained loudly about it. The armored car was much smaller than armored cars would become once people began to build them that way from scratch. It was top-heavy on its leaf springs even without the little pillbox on the roof of the box. It would have looked funny if the muzzle of a Maxim machine gun hadn't been sticking out of the turret.

The crew was too slick to drive with their carbide headlights lit but they were dumb to be driving that fast by moonlight. The driver could no doubt make out the twin ruts of the wagon trace and was depending on them to act like railroad tracks in the shady places.

Since Roman chariots had started out with a four-foot-eight gauge, every wagon, railroad train, and now horseless carriage built by western Europeans or their colonists had the same wheel gauge. Thus, the wagon trace was deeply rutted to fit the tires as the armored vehicle followed them, or thought it was.

Captain Gringo had of course told his men to dig where a wild fig tree spread its inky shadows across the trace. The driver didn't slow down for one lousy island of shade. He should have. The right-hand wheels broke through the dust-covered twigs covering the knee-deep slit trench dug along one rut. Since the other rut was still solid, the armored motorcar flopped over on its side with a tinny crash, slid in a cloud of dust, screams, and curses, and came to rest with two wheels spinning up at the moon as the dust began to settle.

Captain Gringo waited as the echoes faded. The driver opened the door facing the sky and stuck his head out to see if he could climb out. He could have, but then somebody blew his brains out with a carbine and all hell broke loose!

"Hold your fucking fire!" shouted Captain Gringo as bullets spanged uselessly off the boiler plate. Morales and Robles were yelling the same thing up and down the line. So as the fusillade faded, sheepishly, Captain Gringo jumped over the rock and advanced on the careened vehicle. Before he could get to it, the trapdoor of the turret, now facing him, opened. He fired into the black opening as a hand grenade came out to bound like a bunny across the red clay at him. He caught it with the toe of his boot, really just trying to get it the hell away from him before it went off. But, as luck would have it, he kicked it right back into the turret. So it exploded inside!

He grinned and said, "I'll be damned!" as he moved closer, out of the line of fire from the hatch, as blue smoke rose from it to drift lazily away in the moonlight. He got to the vehicle, stood to one side of the open hatch, and called, "I've got a grenade of my own. Throw out your guns and follow them before I count three!"

He counted to three. Nothing happened. Robles ran up to him and asked what happened next. Captain Gringo said, "One of your men fired too soon. So you get to look inside, you trigger-happy sonofabitch!"

Robles sighed, "That is not just. I shot him for doing that. He was the man who raped that *puta* back there. I told him what you said, but some people just don't listen."

Then Robles struck a match and looked inside. He whistled and said, *"Ay caramba!* There were three of them. They are all in the condition I like to see *rurales*—bloody and dead. Shall I see about salvaging their weapons and the contents of their pockets before we burn this creation?"

Captain Gringo said, "We're not going to destroy it if it still runs. Haul the bodies out and hide them in the brush. Then see if you and the guys can lever it back up-right. Use some of Morales's squad if you have to, but do it pronto!"

He returned to Pilar. The girl was chewing on her

kerchief like a locked-up pup chews a slipper. He said, "It's over. You can get up now. But be ready to duck, just in case I'm wrong."

He sat on the rock and lit a smoke as he added, "I've been thinking about how we're to get you home. The railroad's a long way to walk, but if we can get that horseless carriage to run, we can have you in San Blas in no time."

"But, Ricardo, Carmencita said *los rurales* are patrolling the coast road!"

"Yeah. Maybe she lied. Maybe she told the truth. I hate inconsistent dames."

With the gang of guerrillas putting their backs into it, they had the armored motorcar on its wheels and backed out of the trap in no time. Captain Gringo rose, helped Pilar to her feet, and said, "Let's see if we can crank her up again. Do you know how to drive a horseless carriage?"

"Are you serious? I never saw one of the things before that one drove up to my *casa* the other day. That was when they arrested my servants. They had two motor vehicles. One was an open truck to carry *rurales* and another to carry my people away."

Captain Gringo led her to the armored motorcar. His men were standing around, grinning. He didn't have to count noses to see that even after Robles had shot one idiot, he had too many people to stuff in the vehicle. He climbed up the side and dropped into the turret. By moonlight through the open hatch he saw the grenade had only chipped a little paint and splattered a lot of blood on the inner steel walls. He could see the whole construction formed one hollow shell. He saw the driver's seat and steering tiller, forward. He could see how one could get at the engine to the rear from inside. The machine gun was mounted in the slit with a full belt dangling. A crank to the left of the Maxim's breech block turned the turret either way on its circular track. There were extra cases of ammo and a box of grenades racked on either side. A couple of five-liter fuel cans had been securely racked, too, and by some miracle hadn't been punctured by the grenade that had finished off the crew. Things were looking up, if he could start the engine. He stuck his head out and asked, "Do any of you guys know how to drive a motorcar?"

He'd known it was a dumb question when he asked it. But there was always a chance, and he couldn't man the Maxim and drive at the same time.

As they all stared blankly up at him, Captain Gringo said, "That's what I thought. Let's see, we have room for maybe four in here, crowded. Six or seven might be able to ride outside, hanging on a lot. This isn't going to work, gang. Not unless I send one squad home."

Then he cocked his head and hissed, "Everybody take cover! I hear another engine coming from the west!"

He dropped down inside and started cranking like hell as his people ran for cover. He had the gun slit pointed back down the wagon trace and was peering through it along the sights of the machine gun as the brazenly lit headlights of another motor vehicle approached. He muttered, "What the hell? Oh, right, the mop-up crew in the truck. This one was supposed to hit hard with its lights out, and to hell with their own police informers. Then, gunmen following in a thin-skinned truck could fan out through the brush around the ranch house and make sure. I guess it would have worked."

The oncoming truck slowed down as its headlights picked up the stalled armored motorcar on the trace ahead. He said, "Come on. A little closer, dammit! Don't you guys have any curiosity?"

They did. The truck stopped just a few yards away and a voice called out, "What happened? Did you get a flat?"

Captain Gringo aimed just above the headlights and

replied by traversing a burst of Maxim lead across the black bulk outlined by the sky. His guerrillas opened up with their own guns, pumping lead into the truck from their flanking positions. Captain Gringo traversed back, for luck, then called out, "Hold your fire!" He didn't want to put the truck out of action.

Robles was starting to think like him about motor vehicles. So he charged out of the bush, zigzagging, and flattened out against the side of the truck to have a look inside. He called out, "All down, dead or dying, Captain Gringo!"

The tall American put the Maxim on safe and climbed out of his turret, calling back, *"Bueno.* Haul them out before they ooze all over the floorboards. Morales, to me on the double!"

Morales ran up to him, grinning like a mean little kid in the moonlight. Captain Gringo led him around to the rear of the armored motorcar, lit up by the carbide lamps of the shot-up truck. He said, "See this? It's the starting crank. I kicked the lever inside to neutral. That's important. I'll show you that part in a minute. First, let's see if she still runs."

He cranked the engine. It was warm, so it started on the second try. He grinned and said, *"Bueno.* Now we'd better give you some driving lessons. We've got a few minutes."

"Por favor, Captain Gringo! Can it be possible to learn how to drive a horseless carriage in a few minutes?"

"No. But it's all the time we have, and I'm depending on you to drive that other truck down the coast road after me."

Actually, it took over an hour before he had Morales steering well enough to keep the wheels more or less in the ruts as they tooled up and down the wagon trace a few

148

times. By then, the others had the truck bed rubbed fairly clean with dry grass. Robles acted a little hurt that he'd not been offered driving lessons. So Captain Gringo explained, "The girl, you, and a couple of your best men will be riding with me in the lead. I'll let you man the tiller on the straighter stretches as we go, if there's a chance. Morales and most of the guys will follow us in the truck, if it still runs."

It did. As he'd noticed, both vehicles had the same Benz chassis and rear-mounted engines. So, though the truck's dash had some bullet holes in it and the seat was a little sticky, nothing important had been damaged. After putting out the headlights, Morales was able to start it and turn it around without help. Captain Gringo said, "I'll drive slow, at first. Don't follow me too close, but for God's sake keep me in sight." Then he yelled, "Everybody mount up!" and went back to his own stolen vehicle.

As he sat at the tiller beside Pilar, with Robles and a couple of others hunkered behind them on the flat floor under the turret, Robles asked him how he could shoot and drive at the same time. Captain Gringo said, "I can't. So make sure you don't block me if I hit the brakes and come over the back of this seat *poco tiempo!*"

He threw the armored motorcar in gear and lurched it out across the grass in a circle back to the wagon trace. He told one of his men to stand up and see if Morales was following. The guerrilla said he was. Captain Gringo resisted an impulse to give her the throttle. They were moving only a little faster than a man could trot. On the other hand, he didn't want Morales hitting a tree any faster than that.

By the time they reached the mouth of the valley and saw the moonlight on the sea ahead, Captain Gringo was used to the feel of the tiller and, assuming Morales might be, too, speeded up to about ten miles an hour. At his side, Pilar said, "Oh, we are going so fast!" and he said,

"Relax. They drive even faster than this in Paris these days. These gas buggies can do fifteen, even twenty miles an hour."

"Heavens! What is the world coming to? How shall people ever cross the street once these things become popular?"

"Very, very carefully, I suppose. But look on the bright side. Even though they come down the street like horse-drawn buggies whipped to full stride, they take up half the length of a buggy and team. So there'll be fewer traffic jams, most likely, and the cities should smell a lot nicer, without all those horse droppings on the cobbles."

He coasted out onto the main highway, saw it was clear both ways at this hour, and swung south with the moonlit Pacific to their right and the black hills rising to their left. He chuckled and asked, "Isn't this neat? This would be like a romantic carriage ride in the country if we were going a little slower and knew no *rurales* were around the next bend in the road."

She said, "Nobody will ever take girls for romantic rides in these things, silly! What girl could feel romantic with her hair being blown and her, ah, nether parts being bounced so?"

"I guess you're right. Would you like to take the tiller, Pilar?"

"At this speed? With sea cliffs just to the side?"

"Slide your hand under mine. I'll guide you till you get the feel of it. Come on, Pilar. This could be important."

She gingerly put her left hand on the tiller between them as he slid his hand over hers. He still guided as she got the feel of it. Her hand felt cool and a lot nicer than the tiller handle. He felt her confidence growing and eased up his own pressure. Then he grabbed harder as he warned, "You're overcontrolling. This is not a handful of reins, Pilar. You don't have to neck-rein a motor vehicle to make it turn. Think of it as a very responsive cow pony that only needs a hint, see?"

She did, and as she started steering better, she said, "This is fun! I did not think it would be so easy to steer this thing. You are right, it does not have a mind of its own, like a horse. It is most obedient, no?"

"Yeah, but on the other hand, you can't depend on it to sidestep any bumps, and it'll run right into a tree a horse would walk around no matter what you did with the reins. Put your foot on my instep and feel. I may as well teach you how to brake, just in case. This lever, here, is the throttle. It stays where you set it, so you don't have to worry about it. I'm not up to teaching you about the gears or spark lever just yet. If I can teach you to hold her on the road or to stop when I yell to, we'll be ahead of the game."

He was aware of Robles glaring at the backs of their heads, so he laughed and said, "I know I told you I'd show you how to drive, Robles. Later. You can shoot a gun better than a pretty girl, and, what the hell, she'll be getting off soon."

Robles didn't answer. Pilar said, "You can't leave me anywhere, Ricardo! I have no money. I have no friends in San Blas. What would I do alone there? I am not the sort of woman who can sell herself for money in a seaport, and I have nothing else to sell!"

He said, "We'll drop you off well this side of town. Don't walk in before daybreak. By then it should be over whether we're alive or not. I just went through the boxes in back. Here—take this and stuff it somewhere it won't show."

He reached into his side pocket with his free hand and put the roll of bills in her lap, adding, "Relax, Robles. There's plenty left for you and yours. Apparently the guys who drove this thing collected the egg money for their *rurale* captain. They had a whole ammo box

151

stuffed with bills and some poor bastard's gold teeth. We can spare a lady train fair home."

Pilar picked up the roll with her free hand and gasped, "My God, how shall I ever be able to repay you, Ricardo? There must be a thousand pesos here!"

"More like fifteen hundred. Why should you worry about paying us back? It's not *our* money. Buy yourself a new hat or something with the change."

He heard Robles unsnapping the metal box in back. He said, "*That* comes later too. I want the loot shared evenly among the men. You and Morales get time and a half, of course."

"That is most generous Captain Gringo. What about your share?"

"I don't want any. My comrade back in camp and I have enough to buy drinks, smokes, and railroad tickets, if nobody's shooting at us at the time. I'm trying to encourage you guys to make that possible."

The man standing with his head out the turret hatch called down, "I see lights in the road ahead!"

Captain Gringo peered through the slit ahead of him and slowed down as he made them out a few seconds later. He said, "Looks like a checkpoint. Some guys with guns standing between a fire on either side of the road. Hang on, kiddies. They don't look like *rurales*. Those are *federale* uniforms. The army's getting into the act."

"Are we going to run the roadblock, Captain Gringo?" asked Robles, adding, "They can't hurt us in this thing."

Captain Gringo said, "They can sure hurt the guys behind as in that open truck. *Silencio*. The next few minutes may get tricky."

He braked to a stop a pistol shot from the troopers and missed, "Out of the way!" as he rolled over the back of the seat and elbowed his way up into the turret. A noncom stepped out in the road and called out. "Hey, *rurales*. Why you stop there? Come closer and show us your trip ticket, eh? We have no instructions about you guys."

Captain Gringo opened up with the machine gun, feeling almost sorry for the *federales* as he chopped them down, whether they ran, fired back, or just stood there, until all eight of them lay twitching in the firelight.

He stuck his head up out of the hatch and saw Morales had stopped in hailing range. He yelled, "Detail some men to shove those bodies out of sight over the cliff. Then kick out those fires."

He tapped the man nearest him in the turret and said, "You, take your machete and shinny up one of those poles on the landward side. Hack away the wires. Do it now."

As he made room for the grinning guerrilla to climb out, Robles said, "Ah, I see why you wish the fires out. It will take them until morning to find where we cut the wires. But why are we cutting the wires at all, my captain?"

"Jesus, that's a dumb question, Robles. If we have time, we'll cut some more. They're already expecting us in San Blas. The one thing we have going for us is that they think we're walking! When the line goes dead, they'll start looking for the break way to the north. Before they can compare notes, we should be there and halfway back."

"Ah, *sí*, and with this grand vehicle, we can simply drive into the fort atop Cerro de Basilio and load the truck with guns and ammo for El Aquilar Negro, no?"

"No. That's a dumb question, too. Haven't you figured out by now that they haven't reactivated that old Spanish fort above San Blas?"

Robles gasped, "The thought never crossed my mind! How did you know this thing, Captain Gringo?"

"The thought crossed my mind that if I had a mess of goodies hidden in an old Spanish fort, I'd sort of like to keep it a secret. Police informers keep telling us the stuff is there. El Aquilar Negro was told it was there. By who?

A government official who gossips to rebels a lot? It's an obvious setup, *muchacho*. They tried to bait you guys out of a stronghold they're hesitant to attack by telling you there was a good reason to *come out* and get shot."

"*Madre de Dios*, it is so obvious, once one thinks about it! But, Captain Gringo, if the guns are not in the old fort above San Blas, why are we going to San Blas?"

"To get guns and ammo, of course. Those guys I just shot were *federales*, and the army's just moved into this area in force. Armies need supplies. A lot of supplies. The railroad only carries stuff as far as San Blas. So San Blas is where we'll find their quartermaster depot. Not up on a stupid mountain abandoned as useless years ago. By the railroad tracks where guys like *los federales*, and us, can get at 'em!"

They hit another checkpoint at about three in the morning. This time Pilar, at the tiller, just kept driving while Morales, another quick study, lagged a quarter of a mile back until Captain Gringo simply machine-gunned the roadside troopers, who'd been set up to stop regular road traffic, not armored vehicles that bore down on them spitting automatic fire.

Captain Gringo liked to vary his methods to confuse the other side. So he didn't stop to clean up or cut wires. Less than an hour later, still riding up in the turret, he saw he might have made a mistake. Ahead, in the moonlight, he saw a whole troop of cavalry coming up the road! He growled, "Smart thinking. The guys back there were supposed to check in from time to time by wire, and they missed an all's-well, right?"

The cavalry troopers spotted the armored motorcar at about the same time. Whatever they'd been riding hard to intercept, it hadn't been a horseless carriage bearing down at them at twenty miles an hour!

They reined in and an officer yelled to dismount and take cover. Not the smartest thing he could have yelled on a narrow road hemmed in by a rock wall on one side and a sea cliff on the other.

The smart riders wheeled their mounts and headed south at full gallop as Captain Gringo opened up with the Maxim, blowing horses and riders to hash on the road or sending them off the cliff to the sea-washed rocks below.

As Pilar steered around a fallen horse and the rider, the top-heavy armored vehicle swayed dangerously. He called down, "Run *over* the bastards, and let's have some more speed! We can't let any get away!"

So Pilar swallowed hard and opened the throttle, whimpering with fear as she clung to the tiller with both hands and tried to keep them on the road. She scared the hell out of Captain Gringo, too. But he saw they were gaining on the wise-asses who'd retreated down the road ahead. They were doing at least thirty and swaying like a steel ship in a heavy sea as he stuck to his gun and proceeded to empty saddles as they overtook them. As he spilled the last rider over the edge of the sea cliff, horse and all, Captain Gringo dropped down and yelled, "Slow down! We're coming to a curve!"

Pilar wailed that she didn't know *how* to slow down! Then she stood on the brakes with both feet, and at least they were sliding instead of rolling when they hit the rail of boulders some thoughtful road builders had put along the curve. A couple of rocks rolled down the slope to the sea below, but they stayed on the road, with the front wheels on the very edge of the drop.

He climbed over beside her and threw the gears in reverse, saying, "Good girl. I knew I could bank on you."

Pilar didn't answer. She'd buried her face in her hands and started to bawl. Behind him, one of the men was crying, too.

Captain Gringo backed to safety, then squinted out the slit on Pilar's side and saw that Morales, in the truck, had made it this far, too. He grinned and reversed gears again to continue on their way.

It was almost dawn when they passed through a little seaside village. It wasn't on his map, but Pilar remembered it from her trip up from San Blas with her late husband. She said they were about three miles from San Blas itself. He braked to a stop on the far side of town and said, "Okay, doll. There was a light over the door of a posada back there. Walk back and tell them your mount threw you and that you'll wait there until the morning stage arrives. Don't show them your Wad. Haggle for food and a seat by the door. The southbound stage won't get here before full light. Act surprised if you hear anything about us, either way. Make sure it's all over before you go to the depot for your ticket home. Go with God, *muchacha,* and have a nice life."

He reached across her to open the steel door on her side. She sobbed, "You do everything so suddenly, Ricardo! Is this really adios? I can't believe it!"

He kissed her, then shoved her out. She was crying as he pulled the door shut, threw the vehicle in gear, and drove on, saying, "Robles, get your fat ass next to mine and let's see if I can teach you to steer in the next couple of miles."

Robles chuckled and said, "I think that one liked you, Captain Gringo."

The American shrugged and said, "I liked her, too. But there's a time and place for everything. Put your hand on this tiller. I'll hold your wrist till you get the feel of it. Damn, you have ugly hands, Robles."

"Your great paw does nothing for me, either. But I am

beginning to see why you northerners do not march with *adelitas*. Marching with such uncivilized people must be very frustrating, especially at night around the fire. But I must say we made better time than anyone in Mexico would have considered at all possible!"

"That's the general idea, Robles. You guys would still own Texas if Santa Anna hadn't given Houston a couple of extra days to set up at San Jacinto. Your general had more guns, more men, probably the same guts. But he didn't like to sleep alone and he didn't like forced marches. So he rode to battle in a carriage with a sixteen-year-old mistress and a wagon train of luxuries, slow, while a mess of desperate and doubtless less comfortable Texans dug themselves in, just in time."

"You do not have to rub it in, Captain Gringo. I said I got the point. Where are we going to hide these vehicles when we get to San Blas? I do not know the town."

"That makes two of us. We'd better ask directions. I see buildings ahead, so we must be there. You're on your own. Steady as she goes while I get back up in the turret."

As he started to climb out of his seat, Robles said, "Hey, not so fast! I do not know how to stop this thing!"

"We're going slow. Just run it into something solid and it should stop. But don't stop unless I tell you to, right?"

He left the cursing Robles at the steering tiller and stuck his head out the top. He saw Morales in the truck behind and waved him closer. As the truck got within shouting distance, Captain Gringo yelled, "You don't know nothing. You just work for me, and I'm working for our beloved *el Presidente!* Got that?"

Morales beeped the bulb of his tin horn twice. Captain Gringo laughed and turned to face forward. The buildings were rising on either side now. He called down to Robles, "Swing inland at the first broad street. There has to be a civic center some damned place."

157

He saw he'd guessed right when they turned the corner and he spotted an imposing customs house of lava blocks with a plaza beyond. A couple of men in uniform were standing out front. They gaped as they saw what had just turned the corner. He cupped his hands to his mouth to shout, "Hey, which way to that army depot? We need gasolino!"

One of them pointed the way they were going and shouted back, "By the railroad depot, that way. Are you guys army?"

"Hell, no, can't you see we're desperadoes?"

They laughed, the dumb bastards.

Robles had heard the exchange and steered them along one side of the plaza. There was an old church one way and a newer cluster of functional stucco buildings dead ahead. In case anyone was lost, a handy sign on a lamp post had an arrow and was lettered 39TH QUARTER-MASTER DEPOT.

Robles could read. So he simply followed the arrow until they saw a gate ahead. There was a sentry box and, of course, a sentry came out to stand in the center of the road, gun across his chest at port arms. Robles didn't know how to stop. So he didn't. The guard yelled, "Are you *loco en la cabeza?*" as he leaped out of the way at the last minute and fell on his ass. Captain Gringo didn't want to make more noise than he had to. So as the guy started to get up, he just shot him with his .38.

It wasn't silent enough. As they drove into the depot, doors started opening and *soldados* came boiling out as, somewhere, a bugle sounded. The tall American in the turret shrugged, dropped behind the Maxim, and squeezed the trigger with one hand while he spun the turret around and around with his crank in the other. The turret began to reek of cordite and hot brass, but he wasn't nearly as unhappy about that as the quartermaster troops he was smoking up. So the ones who could still stand staggered back inside the barracks to shoot at him from cover. He called down, "Robles, steer over there and see if you can run me along those windows! Close! Scrape the bricks!"

Then he told one of the others riding with him to hand up the grenades one at a time. Robles drove in a circle, swung toward the barracks, and as a bullet spanged off the steel armor, point-blank, Captain Gringo began to heave grenades, blind, with his head safely down. Some of them hit brick and bounced off to explode behind them on the hard-packed dirt. Others went through windows, where they did a lot more damage. Robles got to the end, swung away, and circled back as Captain Gringo, out of grenades, covered the gaping glassless windows with the muzzle of his Maxim. There was nobody peeking out just now, so he held his fire. He called down, "Robles, step on that brake pedal and see what happens." So Robles did. They slid to a stop and, since they were in gear, killed the engine.

Then sudden eerie silence was broken by Morales driving in through the gate. He stopped nearby, his own engine running, and called out for some instructions.

Captain Gringo yelled, "Those crates piled by the tracks—get over there, bust 'em open, and load all the ammo you can find. Machine guns, if they got 'em. Don't worry about smaller arms. I'm covering you here, so move it!"

Morales drove away, beeping his horn. This time Captain Gringo didn't think it was funny. They could get at the engine from inside their armor. But the damned fool who'd designed this thing had left the starting crank on the outside, and Robles had stalled broadside to the barracks!

Captain Gringo dropped down inside, adjusted the spark and gears, and said, "I have to go out and crank. If I don't make it, do the best you can, *muchacho*."

"No, you are too valuable, Captain Gringo. Let me! It was my fault we stalled, no?"

"No, it was mine. I ordered you to stop," sighed Captain Gringo, opening the door on his side. It was the safe side, so nobody could hit him until he got to the rear. Then he took a deep breath, stepped out in the open, and grabbed the crank, growling, "One crank's all you get baby!"

But it took three, and then, as the engine caught on, someone in the barracks caught on and bounced paint and lead confetti in his hair as he ducked back around the tank, muttering, "I'll get you for that!"

But when he got back up behind the machine gun, he saw nothing but a haze of gunsmoke in one window. He fired a short burst through it to let them know he had them zeroed in. Then he called down to one of his men, "Let me know when Morales starts back. What are they up to right now?"

"They are putting boxes on the truck, my captain. But how long can we safely stay here?"

Another bullet spanged off the turret. Captain Gringo put a burst through that window, too, and called down, "Who said it was safe here now? We stay till we go. Uh-oh, some guys never learn!"

This time, when he fired, he caught the first sniper just as he was propping his rifle over the window sill. The *federale*'s head exploded in a cloud of red mist.

The belt was about used up, too. Captain Gringo reached down for another and just had it threaded in when he heard two beeps and his lookout said, "Morales is coming, my captain!"

Captain Gringo yelled, "Robles, move that lever to your left and circle when she starts crawling forward. The throttle's set. Try and keep between the truck and that damned barracks as we pull out." And then, not waiting

160

for an answer, he cranked the turret around to cover his other vehicle.

Nobody bothered them as they drove out side by side. But when they reached the plaza at least a regiment of *soldados* were milling there in confusion as their officers and noncoms tried to line them up and get a handle on the situation.

Captain Gringo didn't give them the chance. As he traversed hot machine-gun lead back and forth, aiming low to do as much damage as possible with flying stone splinters and screaming hot ricochets, the plaza cleared miraculously. Partly, anyway. Most of the already-mixed-up *soldados* ran for cover. But a lot still lay where they'd dropped.

He signaled Morales to fall back and follow as the armored motorcar took the lead out of town. He changed the belt again, dropped down, and reached over Robles to open the throttle. Robles gasped, "I can't control her at this speed, dammit!" But Captain Gringo said, "Try," and climbed back up in the turret. He saw what Robles meant as they rocked from side to side with Robles over-controlling from curb to curb as they tore back the way they'd come. As they rounded the curve to the coast road on two wheels, some guys in *federale* uniform were rolling a wagon out onto the road to block it. Captain Gringo opened up on them with the Maxim just before Robles, having no choice in the matter, plowed into the wagon at thirty or so. As they tore on through the cloud of flying kindling, the American laughed and said, "Remind me never to try that against a boiler-plated horseless carriage!"

The road ahead seemed clear but winding, so he dropped down beside Robles, took the tiller, and said, "Nice going. The idea is to stay more or less in the center of the lane, though."

Robles made the sign of the cross and said, "You are crazy! We had heard you were crazy before you joined us. But nobody said you were *really* crazy! For God's sake, slow down!"

"Later. Morales is crazy too, and we'd better put some road between us and whatever they have to chase us with."

They whipped past the posada he'd told Pilar to stay in. He didn't see her in the doorway. He was glad, he guessed. Jesus, she'd been a pretty little thing. But a guy couldn't expect to win 'em all.

As they reached open country again, Robles said, "If you won't slow down, will you at least tell me where we are going? This road does not go all the way to Mazatlán, and *los rurales* are headquartered in Rosario, where this road ends."

"That's where we're going. We'll need mules to transport all the stuff we stole over the mountains to the stronghold. The map says Rosario is only about seventy or eighty kilometers from El Aquilar Negro's camp, as the crow flies. We'll pick us some pack mules there and . . ."

"Pick up *whose* pack mules?" Robles cut in, adding, "Didn't you hear what I just said? *Los rurales,* a whole company of *los rurales,* holds Rosario! No peons there will have any animals for us. *Los rurales* even steal the pigs and chickens!"

"I've noticed that. There should be a big corral somewhere near *rurale* headquarters. Do you know where that is?"

"Of course. But are you talking about stealing the mules we need from the corral of *los rurales?*"

"Why not? We need mules, and I wouldn't want to let the motherfuckers feel left out, would you?"

Robles smiled grimly and said, "You paint pretty pictures, for a madman. But it won't work. By now they know we stole these two vehicles from them. We won't be able to simply drive in, boldly, as we did back there."

"Yeah, I know. We're going to have to do it some other way."

"Ah, you have a way, then, Captain Gringo?"

"Not yet. I'm still working on it. But what the hell, it's going to take us a while to get there, right?"

In Mexico City, *el Presidente* Diaz was not enjoying his breakfast. It was a nice breakfast. Few of his subjects could have afforded it, or the pretty young woman seated across from him in a see-through black lace dressing gown. But *el Presidente* still had heartburn. He glared up at his uniformed aide and said, "There is only one possibility. I thought when those first reports came in that our informants were confused about the names. I thought Captain Gringo and that damned little Frenchman used aliases and that they, Duran, and Tio Pancho were all the same bastards. Now I see we have at least four, not just two, soldiers of fortune to deal with. Their friends are good, too. Has anyone figured out exactly how many rebels hit our depot in San Blas?"

"*Sí el Presidente.* From the damage and casualties, they make it out at least a full battalion attacking far from where we thought they were holed up above Mazatlán!"

"A full battalion, in two vehicles? Never mind, if Captain Gringo led the attack, they doubtless *thought* it was a full battalion!"

Diaz got to his feet and began to pace in his bathrobe as the mistress and aide watched, respectfully silent. The Liberator could order *anyone* shot when he was in a pacing mood!

The white-haired dictator stopped, turned, and snapped, "Wait. If Walker and Verrier hit San Blas, they can't be

163

with the rebels above Mazatlán. Duran and that other soldier of fortune can't be as good as the real thing. I'd have heard from them before if they were half as good. I keep an eye open for real talent. Damn, I wish those boys would work for *me!* But, no matter, the point is they are not with El Aquilar Negro, either. Are we in direct communication with the column I sent up into the hills after El Aquilar Negro's band?"

"More or less, sir. We have runners as well as direct communication with Mazatlán."

"*Bueno.* Signal a change in orders. I knew from our spies where the camp was, but, being prudent not to take on too great a force, I told them to circle and move in carefully. But Captain Gringo and Gaston Verrier are not there. Our spies say El Aquilar Negro is sick and helpless. Order our men to advance boldly and wipe out the camp before those more dangerous soldiers of fortune can possibly get back! After they take the stronghold, they are to tidy up and set a trap for that crazy *Yanqui* and his French companion. What is the latest on those American navy men?"

"Another *Yanqui* ship is coming to pick them up, *el Presidente.* It is my understanding that their intelligence officer and a shore patrol mean to stay behind and search for the escapees. They wished to accompany our column, but of course I relayed your orders not to let them."

"*Bueno.* I do not like to have visitors returning to the outside world with tales about my methods. *Los Yanquis* are so silly about the women and children of unimportant people. Send word to let the gringo shore patrol come up and identify the bodies after Captain Gringo and his Frenchman are dead. Not before. What are you waiting for? Can't you see I'm having breakfast?"

The aide saluted, spun on his heels, and left. Diaz sat down at the table again and sighed. "I don't know. I think I may be getting an ulcer. It used to be so much fun to run a country. But nobody seems to understand how much I've done for Mexico, and outsiders meddling with my rebels really puts me off my feed. I can handle children like El Aquilar Negro without getting out of bed. But that Captain Gringo is unsettling as a mad dog running loose in my house. I must be getting old. I used to *enjoy* crossing swords with a master. Now it just gives me a stomachache."

"You are not old, my hero," she replied, slipping out of her chair to crawl to him, open his robe, and lower her head to his lap. He sighed and ran his hand through her hair as she began to suck. Then he said "No, child. I know you mean well, but I'm too worried right now!"

Later, up in the Sierras above Mazatlán, Gaston was worried, too. He'd done his best to whip the guerrillas into shape. They were a hell of a lot better than when he'd started. But he still wasn't ready to pit them against a band of determined bloomer girls. He was sure the new feminist movement had more real fighters in its ranks. These *pobrecitos* now at least moved when he told them to move and then watched them to see that they did. But he couldn't be everywhere at once. The stronghold was too spread out to set up a decent perimeter, and when he'd ordered them to move up to one end of the valley and dig in, some snitch had run crying to El Aquilar Negro and the delirious, useless leader had countermanded the idea.

Gaston heard a shrill whistle as he hunkered in the meager shade of a rock on the ridge east of camp. He turned to see Felicidad coming up the slope. The girl flopped beside him and said, "Our lookout atop the potato rocks to the east says he sees dust to the west. You said if they attacked before Captain Gringo and the others get back, they will hit us from the east, no?"

Gaston said, "I still say so, my worried beauty. I have a map of the hills all around etched in my *fantastique* brain, in ink. I used to serve in the Mexican army. Before that, I fought them as a Legionnaire. Don't tell anyone, but Mexicans are smarter. What the lookout saw to the west was the dust of a dispatch rider. If your spies are correct, and a column of *federales* is moving in after failing to trap our friends to the south, which I could have told them was impossible, they will not be allowed to raise dust. They will have dismounted and they will move in on foot, as usual. *Los federales* are good dragoons. They know better than to try cavalry charges over hog-back ridges and through boulder fields sloping at crazy angles. *Mais non,* if they intend to do it at all, they will do it *right!* They have El Aquilar Negro down as an untrained bandit leader, which is only just, when you think about it. They will expect him to prepare for an attack from the west, as unskilled military minds are prone to assume. Ergo, they will attack from those higher hills, over that way. Trust me. I, Gaston, am never wrong."

"You were wrong about how soon they would be arriving. Both you and my Deek said it would not be for days."

"Girls do not have dicks, but no matter. I confess we assumed we were up against the usual cautious mind of a sensible professional. Since your spies from town tell you a battalion of manic *federales* marched over the coast hills with orders to get right to it, I take it on faith they mean to throw *some* caution to the wind. No doubt they have heard that your leader is ill and your best men are not here. Nonetheless, *federale* officers are not picked for stupidity. Knowing our location, they may advance with uncharacteristic boldness. Nonetheless, they will want to attack in a manner offering them the advantage, *hein? Eh bien,* to the west, the approaches are *très* steep. The few men I posted on that side have *très* formidable cover. The reason I have most of our so-called *soldados* on this ridge with me is because, as anyone can see, it's *très* lousy. The slopes to our east are gentle. The next ridge to the east is higher. If they mass behind it, dust us with artillery, and make a determined downhill charge ... ah, well, we shall doubtless beat them back at least once or twice. After that, I promise nothing. You are pretty, Felicidad. When the shooting starts, you and the other pretty girls had better run over the western ridge and make yourselves scarce, *hein?*"

"Never! I have spoken to the other *adelitas*. We too are armed and dangerous. We mean to fight shoulder to shoulder with you *hombres!*"

Gaston grimaced and said, "I wish you would not. It unsettles a green *soldado* to see a woman hit nearby. As it is, I expect half of them to run as soon as they see the enemy. Can't you girls find something better to do?"

She stuck out her lower lip and said, "We are determined to man the front line!"

"That is a contradiction in terms. But if you have to *woman* some line or other, you have my permission to set up on the ridge across the valley."

"But you said nobody was liable to attack from that direction!"

"*Oui,* but you said they might. Tell your savage Amazons to dig in and keep their heads down as we guard each other's rears, *hein?*" He laughed and added, "Speaking of rears, you said something about a friend of yours who admires older men, remember?"

"*Si.* If we live through the battle, I will introduce you to her. I must go now. There is so much to do if we girls are to be prepared in time."

He watched her fondly as she scampered down the

slope. He wished there were some way to leave women, horses, and other pretty creatures out of wars. If she and the other girls were on the far side when things got bad, at least they'd have a chance of getting away. He knew that was more than he could say. He muttered to himself, "Really, Gaston, my old and wiser, this is no time to consider promises, even to Dick! Oh, I know he's depending on you to hold here until he gets back. But he's an idiot, too! This position is hopeless, the men are worthless, El Aquilar Negro did not have a chance even before he came down with the fever, and what do we owe him? Surely not our lives!"

He grimaced, stood up, and started walking the ridge to make sure every man was in place. He knew it really didn't matter. But he had said he would try.

Getting rid of the stolen vehicles was no problem. Packing all the loot was going to be the problem. Less than an hour's hike south of Rosario, Captain Gringo ran the vehicles up a wooded ravine, emptied the truck, and stripped the armored motorcar of its machine gun, ammo, and grenades. Then he and Morales drove back to the coast road, saw nobody coming either way, and sent the two vehicles over the edge of the cliff to vanish at sea with a pair of mighty splashes.

Now came the hard part. Leaving Morales, the supplies, and most of the men in the ravine, Captain Gringo took Robles, four scouts, and the machine gun farther into the chaparral to see if they could scout the *rurale*-held village without being spotted.

They could. They ran into a young goatherd and his goats on a north-south ridge. He called out, *"Viva la revolución!"* even before they could ask him his political

168

persuasion. So Captain Gringo knew he was a smart kid and enlisted him on the spot as a guide.

He told the goatherd to leave his damned goats where they were and told Robles to kill him if he made a break for it. Then he had the goatherd lead them along the ridges to a saddle overlooking Rosario.

They had a neat bird's-eye view from up here. The village lay by an inlet with an offshore bar forming a natural harbor. The goatherd said most of the people were fishermen. It was just as well. *Los rurales* could use only so much fish. As Captain Gringo had hoped, the *rurale* corrals lay south of the village, beside the highway they patrolled. But then the bastards had gotten even smarter and built their headquarters between said corrals and an easy romp south. The solidly built semifort controlled all entry and exit from Rosario. The goatherd said no pretty girl or man with a gold watch could get in and out of Rosario these days, since the route north to Mazatlán was blocked by mountain spurs running out into the sea.

Captain Gringo stared thoughtfully up that way. On the horizon he could see purple mountains getting their feet wet. Closer in, he saw the smoke plume of a vessel moving their way, fast, with a bone of white water in its teeth. It was a gunboat—American, by her lines. It figured that someone had picked up those seamen stranded in Mazatlán by now.

Turning his attention back to the business at hand, Captain Gringo gazed down at the *rurale* post. The slopes running down to it from here were steep and, thanks to the damned goats, covered with dusty scrub instead of the natural vegetation these hills should have had. He asked Robles what he thought. Robles said, "We could most probably slip down to the corrals without getting shot. We could most probably gather some mules to ride and lead south without getting shot. Getting them out of the corrals past that outpost without getting shot is impossible. Even if most of *los rurales* are out bothering people, there are always some left behind to guard the post. Those walls are thick. Those loopholes are narrow. There is no cover around the place within carbine range. Not even your machine gun would be able to make much of an impression on that place. But the noise would surely bring every *rurale* within kilometers."

Captain Gringo nodded, but asked the goatherd if he knew how many *rurales* there were to worry about down there. The kid said about a dozen. Most of the company had headed north into the mountains at dawn for some reason. The route over the spurs toward Mazatlán was supposed to be impassable. But *rurales* had ridden that anyway.

Captain Gringo nodded and told Robles, "There's always a way. And we don't have much time. The only reason those guys would have to ride for Mazatlán would be if someone told them to. They've been sent to beef up God knows who, to attack the stronghold!" He asked the goatherd if he'd seen any *federales* from his hilltop range. The kid nodded and said a steamer carrying army troops had stopped at Rosario the day before. Captain Gringo swore and said, "That ties it. If we abandon the fresh supplies and ammo, we could just about leg it back to the stronghold in time to get in on the fighting."

Robles said, "But, Captain Gringo, if we go back without ammo, what will we fight with?"

"Yeah, meanwhile it would take at least a couple of shells to reduce that post down there, and this Maxim only fires .30-30s."

He saw the gunboat was close now. The skipper must have been a curious cuss. He was steaming a lot closer to shore than Captain Gringo would have. They were passing Rosario just outside the bar. He could make out the Stars and Stripes and faces gawking shoreward on the bridge. It was probably dull, looking at most of Mexico from out there. A village of whitewashed walls and red tile roofs was apparently worth going out of one's way to see. Captain Gringo snapped his fingers and said, "That's it!" Then he said, "Everybody on the far side of this saddle and keep your heads down!"

He followed, flopped on his belly with the dismounted machine gun angled skyward over the ridge, and muttered to himself, "Let's see. Forty-five degrees is too much. There, *that* ought to do her."

Meanwhile, out on the gunboat, the skipper was watching with some disdain as Lieutenant Carson scanned the shoreline with his binoculars. They'd been told to cooperate with Intelligence. But Carson wasn't showing much intelligence, in the skipper's opinion. Even if the men Carson was hunting were skipping down along the coast road in broad daylight, what the hell were they supposed to do about it? There was no place a deep-draft gunboat could put it, this side of San Blas.

Something thudded solidly on the steel plate roofing of the wheelhouse. It was followed by a burst of five more solid bangs. The skipper blinked and said, "Jesus, we seem to be under fire!"

Another burst of automatic fire fell short, off their port bow. It gave the men on the bridge a line on where it was coming from. The skipper swore, picked up his speaking tube, and ordered battle stations.

In an era of gunboat diplomacy, vessels flying the Stars and Stripes were not allowed to be used for target practice. By this time Carson had ducked below the armored sill of the bridge wing, but he'd ranged on the mystery bursts, too, and yelled, "They're firing on us from that fortresslike whatever just south of town!"

The skipper said, "Teach your granny how to suck eggs! Fire Control! I want a salvo on that blockhouse two points aft my port beam, and I want it *now!*"

171

The gunboat tingled all over as both turrets belched smoke and flame from opposite ends of the gray super-structure. Gunners who enforced gunboat diplomacy got a lot of practice, so they were good. As their shells lanced down through the tile roof of the *rurale* post and blew said roof to red confetti rising on mushroom clouds of brown cordite smoke, the skipper ordered, "Give 'em another salvo! I'll show the bastards, for chipping my paint!"

On shore, Captain Gringo waited, watching with de-light, as the U.S. Navy blew the shit out of the *rurale* post for him. The livestock in the corrals down there were milling wildly in panic as roof tiles fell among them. But the corral walls held. Captain Gringo turned to his men and said, "Let's go! The shelling's stopped!" and, suiting action to his words, charged over the ridge and down the hill with his Maxim braced on his hip.

Later in the day, at the stronghold, Gaston blinked in surprise as he heard the crackle of small-arms fire. There was nobody visible on the slopes to the east. The fire was coming from the west, where nobody was supposed to be dumb enough to attack!

Some of the others Gaston had posted on the east ridge started to rise. Gaston yelled, "Hold your positions! It may be a ruse! Noncoms, see your squads stay in place here. I'll find out what species of idiocy is taking place over there!"

It took Gaston a few minutes to traverse the valley to where Felicidad and the other *adelitas* had taken their positions in what Gaston had assumed to be a foolish girls' errand. Fortunately, the rebel *adelitas* were a lot tougher than they looked. They got to carry guns and ammo a lot, and since women are curious by nature, most of them had demanded and received permission from their *soldados* to fire said guns once in a while.

The *federales* and *rurales* attacking up the steep slope from the west were, as Gaston had foretold, at considerable disadvantage. Their leaders had been as smart as Gaston. They would never have hit the rebel stronghold so directly, had it been up to them. But they had orders from *el Presidente* and they'd been told it would be a pushover with El Aquilar Negro out of action and most of the best men gone.

They'd been told wrong. The girls strung out along the ridge proceeded to cut them down with well-aimed rifle fire as they struggled up the slope. By the time Gaston flopped down beside Felicidad to ask her what on earth was going on, the earth below was soaking up a lot of gore. He stared soberly down at the uniformed bodies scattered among the boulders like discarded rag dolls and whistled softly. Felicidad laughed and said, "They are running back down to safety, the cowards! This is fun. I did not know it was so easy to be a *soldado*. I thought one had to be a man to be a hero!"

Gaston said, "Do not get carried away, my little Amazon. You and these other women were not the heroes just now. Those poor bastards down *there* were the heroes! Being a hero can take fifty years off a man's life."

A woman nearby called out, "Felicidad, do you have any bullets you can spare me? I only have two clips left!"

Felicidad called back, "Make sure you make every bullet count, then. I have none to spare, either."

She turned to Gaston and said, "We need more ammunition. As you see, we can hold this ridge if only we can keep shooting. But I must say it takes a lot of ammunition to stop a charge."

Gaston thought, shook his head, and said, "If the enemy leader has the brains of a gnat, he'll try the next time from the other side. My boys over there will need even *more* ammunition, since their position is *très* lousy compared to yours."

Felicidad sighed and said, "It's not fair. Oh, look, they're coming at us again!" and Gaston blinked and gasped, *"Merde alors,* you are right!"

There was no time to make any smart moves. So, as the long ragged line of uniformed government men waded up the slope at them, Gaston propped his own rifle in position with his elbows and called out, "Hold your fire, *muchachas!* Wait until I open up. Then make every shot count!"

At his side, Felicidad complained, "They are almost within range! Why don't you shoot?"

"Because *almost* is not good enough, of course. Keep your pretty head down. You are skylining yourself. Hold your fire. Easy, easy, let them move a little closer. . . ."

"Closer? They are close enough to see the whites of their eyes!"

"That, my child, is the general idea. *Eh bien,* see that idiot with bars on his shoulders? He is mine. Take the noncom to his left. *Now!"*

Their rifles spoke as one. Their targets rolled back down the slope together, too. Some of the enemy were of course firing back as the other *adelitas* opened up all along the ridge. The smarter ones just ran back down the slope as the riflewomen aimed at the closer ones and dropped them among the rocks and other bodies.

Felicidad laughed, changed her clip, and then made a funny little sound as her rifle went off aimed at the sky. Gaston swore, emptied his own rifle into the retreating skirmish line, then rolled over to pick up Felicidad's fallen rifle. When he had it aimed, he saw no likely target. So he looked down at Felicidad.

The girl lay on her side, staring intently at a rock a few inches from her pretty face. A trickle of blood ran out one corner of her mouth. Gaston made the sign of the cross and gently closed her eyes with his fingers.

The other girl who'd asked about ammo crawled over to them, saying she'd used up her last round. She saw Felicidad and asked, "Is she?" and Gaston said, *"Oui,"* as he handed her a clip from his own ammo belt, saying, "Make this last. It's the only one I can spare. I am called Gaston. How are you called, *muchacha?"*

The girl, a woman, really, said, "I am called Rosita. What does it matter now?"

"I may wish to say goodbye properly. You are very attractive, Rosita. I never expected to end my days between two beautiful women, but then, I have always been lucky."

Rosita, who wasn't really all that pretty, but had a great derriere, said, "This is no time for flattery. All three of us will be cadavers if you don't get the others over to this side *poco tiempo!* Do you wish me to run for them?"

He said, "You'd better get off this ridge. But don't bother the *hombres* over there. They will be having their own problems any minute, if the idiot in charge of this attack comes to his senses."

"What if he does not? If they charge up this slope again, I don't think we can stop them with the ammo we have left, Gaston!"

"I know we can't. You'd better move back to safety, Rosita. Try to remember me fondly in days to come, *hein?"*

"I shall fight at your side, Gaston. Poor Felicidad told me about you. Is it true you have chosen no *adelita?* I lost my *soldado* in a raid a month ago."

"Dear heart, this is a very silly time to discuss our possible future relationship. Observe, those insects down the slope are forming up for another charge!"

He made sure he had a round in his chamber as he lay prone by Felicidad's corpse, with Rosita at his other side. As they watched the ominous advance, Gaston muttered, "The bastard in command has little regard for his men, but he must have noticed how ragged that last volley from up here was. All shitting of the bull aside, Rosita, you'd better move back. This does not look good. Unless the other girls have been hiding extra rounds in their hair, I doubt if we can stop them this time!"

"We can try. What are those shiny things they have on their rifles?"

"Bayonets. One forgets you children have hitherto only tangled with *rurales. Eh bien,* if you insist on dying with me, take this pistol. It should stop a couple for you at close range. Save the last bullet for your pretty self. They shall not be gentle with prisoners after taking such heavy casualties, *hein?*"

She didn't answer. Gaston chose another squad leader as his first target and shot off the side of his head. As Rosita and the others opened up, Gaston heard only half of them were firing now.

The oncoming enemy heard this too. Somewhere, a bugle began to blow full charge, so the skirmish line staggered into an uphill run. Some of them were still dropping, but a lot were not. Gaston's hammer clicked on an empty chamber. He reached for another clip. He didn't have one. He'd even given his damned pistol away!

Then, just as Gaston braced himself to rise and run like hell, a Maxim machine gun opened up from somewhere to the south. Gaston blinked and muttered, *"Sacrebleu* and what the hell?" as people on the slope started falling down a lot. The machine gun wasn't firing at the rebels. It was taking the skirmish line on the flank, and cutting hell out of them!

The confused survivors started moving back down the slope as Captain Gringo changed his belt and told Robles, "They'll be retreating through that cleft in the potato rocks. Can you and your squad beat them there with those grenades? *Bueno!* Get going!"

Then, as Robles and his men squirmed away through the boulders, Captain Gringo opened up again on the men running wildly down the corpse-infested slope to his north. He ceased fire with half his belt left. He hadn't force-marched men and mules over the hills this far to waste ammunition.

He waited. At his side, Morales said, "I think they have given up."

"But Captain Gringo said, "Sit tight. I think so too. But Mother War doesn't give her children many bum guesses. Go back and make sure the pack mules are secure. They've had a rough day and gunfire is hard on everybody's nerves. Cover down on me and don't move on until you see me getting away with it."

Morales left him alone. Captain Gringo waited until he heard cheers and saw the red flannel flag of the rebels waving wildly atop the ridge to his right. Since nobody shot the idiot waving it, he figured it was safe to break cover now. He picked up the dismounted Maxim and started legging it up the slope at an angle. When he looked back, Morales and the mules were following. Off to the west, he heard the tinny crumps of grenades going off and knew Robles was on the ball, too.

Gaston and a gal with an okay face and a big ass came part way down the slope to meet him. Gaston said, "It's about time you got here. Did you get the ammo? We just used up half of what we had. They foxed me by attacking the dumb way. It would have worked, too. But, *regardez* all the dead they left behind! This place is going to stink like hell in a little while."

"Yeah, I'll have to talk to the boss about moving camp. Obviously the other side knew all too well where it was. Is Felicidad okay?"

177

Gaston's face fell. Captain Gringo sighed and said, "Shit. What happened, Gaston?"

"She took one at the base of her throat, angled down. At least she never knew what hit her, Dick. You should have seen how she and the other women fought! I still can't believe it, and I was there. This is Rosita. I saw her first. Do not trifle with her. She is a formidable gunfighter!"

Captain Gringo nodded at the Amazon and led the way over the ridge. As he approached the idiot waving the flag, he saw it was El Aquilar Negro in the flesh. He frowned and said, "I see you've recovered from your fever."

The rebel leader grinned boyishly and replied, "*Sí*, just in time to lead my people to victory. Did you fetch my arms and ammunition?"

"Coming on those mules. I'm sure glad to see you so bright-eyed and bushy-tailed. We're going to have to move this camp."

"But why? We just won the battle, Captain Gringo!"

The trail-sore American looked disgusted and didn't answer. Gaston said, "One swallow does not a summer make, nor one battle a victory. We have given them something to ponder before they attack again. But, rest assured, they will return, the right way, with mountain artillery and someone who knows his business better."

El Aquilar Negro shrugged and handed the banner to an aide before he turned away, saying, "We shall discuss the matter further, later. Right now it is time to celebrate my victory!"

As he swaggered downhill toward his camp, Captain Gringo swore and muttered, "His victory? Are you thinking what I'm thinking, Gaston?"

"*Oui*, we used to shoot malingering cowards in the Legion, too. It is amazing how much that improves the health of fever victims. But it is not our place, Dick. The others would probably resent it if a gringo shot their leader. Besides, if you did, you would *automatique* be stuck with leading these children, *hein?*"

"Yeah, and that's the last thing I want. These poor assholes don't have a chance with *anybody* leading them!"

The problem was solved by Robles. El Aquilar Negro was holding court, seated in a camp chair in front of his tent, when Robles and what was left of his squad came up. Robles had lost another man and had himself been creased by a *federale* bullet. But he said the grenades had done a real job in the cleft of the potato rocks. He added, "I left a couple of lookouts there. Some few of the animals got away to run back to Mazatlán with their tails between their legs. I am surprised to see you so recovered, El Aquilar Negro."

Captain Gringo knew better, but he couldn't keep from saying, "Yeah, if he'd bounced out of bed a few minutes sooner he'd have gotten to fight with the *adelitas*."

El Aquilar Negro got to his feet with a scowl and demanded, "Was that a remark about my manhood, Gringo? Do you doubt I was really ill?"

Captain Gringo smiled thinly and met the rebel leader's gaze as he said, "I think you were sick, all right. The idea of a stand-up fight in place of a brag gives many a village bully a tummy ache. I've been comparing notes with the guys you sent on that suicide mission with me, chico. It's odd that none of the raids that band have made have ever been led by you in person. But it's not my gang. So I guess they can go on being dumb if they want to. Gaston and me are leaving. We've done all we can."

El Aquilar Negro roared, "I shall say who leaves and

who does not! I have been insulted! I will not have it! I demand an apology, Gringo! You will take back what you said, or you will die!"

"Okay, do you want to fight me with knives or guns?"

"Fight you?" The rebel leader blanched, adding, "I do not fight like a peon! *Madre de Dios,* I am a general! I am king of these mountains and rebel leader of Estado Sinaloa!"

Robles said, "Not anymore." Then he drew his gun and put three rounds into El Aquilar Negro's plump chest. As the braggart fell at his feet, he turned mildly to the others, gun muzzle smoking, and said softly, *"I am the general. Are there any objections?"*

There was a moment of stunned silence. Then someone threw his hat in the air and yelled, *Viva Generale* Robles!"

The others seemed to think it was a hell of a good idea. So Robles started to reload his revolver as he asked Captain Gringo, "Before you leave us, is there anything we can do for you, *amigo mio?"*

Captain Gringo said, "Yeah. Gaston and I have to rest up before we push back down to San Blas. I'll leave the heavy stuff and show some of your men how to shoot it, if you can spare us a couple of mules."

Robles smiled boyishly and said, "Take mules, take any woman from the band as *adelitas.* Let us give you money and anything else you like. By the beard of Christ, you have earned more reward than we can ever hope to offer you, you crazy *Yanqui cabrón!"*

Captain Gringo smiled and said, "Virtue, and killing guys working for Diaz, is its own reward. When things have settled down, we'll talk about some moves you can have your people make, General Robles. The smartest thing you could do would be to disband. But Mexico needs gallant idiots if it's ever to be free again. Right now, I need some coffee and a warm meal. You could use a bandage for that bullet crease. You've bled enough to show the others how tough you are."

Robles laughed and said, *"Es verdad!* The two of us are the toughest sonsofbitches in all of Mexico, no?"

"Let's not get sickening about it. Gaston and I still have to make it over to Vera Cruz, and there may still be some tough guys left on the other side."

Now that he knew the way, Captain Gringo managed to cut a few corners as he led Gaston over the same route south to San Blas. Riding muleback sure beat walking, too. He was still leg-sore from having done it the hard way. Gaston was exhausted from the night he'd spent with the buxom Rosita before bidding her a tearful farewell.

Captain Gringo was still worried about the other friends they'd left back there. Robles was a good *soldado,* but the odds were still God awesome, even if they made it to the new hideout deeper in the Sierra Madre Occidental. Gaston was used to parting from old comrades in arms. So he was bitching about the modest rewards for their considerable effort.

He brought it up again as they stopped in a clump of trees to rest the mules and catch some shade. Captain Gringo put a hand in his pocket and said, "Oh, I forgot about that. Here—this is your share from the tribute money I found in the armored motorcar."

Gaston stared at the thick wad of peso notes in his hand and said, *"Sacre* goddamn! One of those rebels back there told me the *très* generous Captain Gringo refused to help himself to any loot."

"I lied. Do I look *that* dumb? Aside from building character with guys I'd just met, I figured if nobody knew I was worth robbing, nobody would try. There's always a couple of sneaks in any outlaw band, right?"

Gaston put his wad away with a fond chuckle and said, "Alas, youth and innocence are so fleeting. Where is the trusting child I first met facing a firing squad with me? Can this cynic be the boy we used to have to lecture on the rules of the game down here?"

Captain Gringo smiled back and said, "It took me a while. But I'm learning. Getting shot at and betrayed a lot does wonders for one's education."

They rode on without getting shot at or betrayed, since they made sure nobody spotted them as they stuck to the high timber. They swung inland and forded the Rio Grande de Santiago where it was shallow and uninhabited. Gaston agreed that trying to board a train in San Blas itself right now could be a little noisy. But the train stopped at Tepic, about fifteen miles east of the seaport, and nobody had shot up Tepic lately.

They abandoned their rifles in the woods, rode into Tepic, and stabled the mules at a livery. Then they bought new suits and hats before risking the ticket office at the Tepic depot. The ticket agent said they were in luck. The trains were just starting to run again. Captain Gringo managed to look innocent as the chatty ticket agent explained there'd been a hell of a battle down the line at San Blas but the army had announced a victory and everything was getting back to normal.

They went to mass at the church across the plaza from the depot while they waited for the east-bound train. Captain Gringo had been raised a Protestant and Gaston said he was an atheist, save in tense moments. But how often would *rurales* pester nicely dressed men in church?

Sanctified, they came out when they heard the whistle blowing and timed it so they had to run for the train, in case anyone on the platform was being a pain about I.D. Nobody was. They swung aboard as the train pulled out. As they stood on the platform between cars to get their bearings, they saw the cars to their rear were second-class coach. They'd asked for pullman compartments in Tepic and been turned down. All compartments were booked. Captain Gringo said, "Stay here. We may work something out with the conductor."

They didn't. The conductor was polite when he punched their tickets and pocketed a healthy tip. He said he could see they were caballeros and they could have the run of the train as far as he was concerned but, alas, the compartments were all taken. He added that there was a nice club car to the rear and said, "When we stop at Guadalajara, some first-class passengers may be getting off. I shall keep it in mind you wish to ride in private."

He moved on. Captain Gringo said, "Well, we can't stand here all the way to Guadalajara. That would be as suspicious as chancing the club car."

Gaston said, *"Oui,* but let me scout it first. With this hat, I tend to blend into any crowd. You, alas, are a big blond moose to be recognized for blocks. Uh-oh, someone's coming!"

They stood clear of the sliding door as it opened. It was Pilar Perez! The young widow gasped, "Ricardo! What are you doing aboard this train? I thought I would never see you again!"

"That makes two of us. But let me figure it out. This is the first train out of San Blas since the shoot-up right?"

"Of course. I had to spend some time in a hotel. I must say you made an awful mess back there, Ricardo. They are still cleaning up after you."

"I see you've had a bath and bought a new dress, too. Nice. Did you manage to get a compartment?"

"Naturally. It's an overnight trip to my father's hacienda. I have to change to a coach, of course, and . . ."

"Never mind all that. I've got to stay out of sight till we're at least out of this state. Let's go. Coming, Gaston?"

"Mais non, my children. You two doubtless have things to talk about, while I, the invisible Gaston, had better

183

do some scouting. If you hear shots, keep the door locked. Otherwise, I shall meet you when we have to change trains tonight, up in the high country."

Captain Gringo nodded and turned to follow Pilar to her compartment. Gaston sighed, "Lucky devil," and headed the other way.

There was nobody he knew in the first coach car he entered. It was crowded. A baby was crying and somewhere a chicken was clucking. Gaston moved on to the next car. It was even more crowded. There would have been more room had not an eight-man squad of men in U.S. Navy tropic whites and canvas leggings occupied facing seats, two by two, with Krag rifles braced against their knees.

Gaston kept walking, hoping they would take him for just another well-dressed Mexican as he raised his hands to light an imaginary smoke until he'd passed them. None of them even looked up at him. It was just as well. He recognized a couple of them from the gunboat he'd sunk.

There was a less exciting coach behind the one the sailors occupied. He saw the next, and last was the club car the conductor had mentioned. Gaston didn't go right in. He pulled his hat brim down as he stood on the platform between cars and peered through the dusty glass. He swore softly, then muttered, "But of course!" as he spotted Lieutenant Carson seated at the bar, profiled to Gaston.

The Navy man had changed to civvies again, in an apparent attempt to be sneaky, or perhaps because it was more comfortable to travel that way. Gaston knew Carson well enough to know why none of his enlisted men were drinking with him.

Gaston lit a real smoke as he considered his options. Unlike Captain Gringo, nobody had invited him to a private compartment. Carson might or might not prowl the train. Carson would certainly recognize his escaped prisoner. He'd spent more time gloating over them than had any other member of the crew.

Gaston made sure nobody was coming either way. Then he got a good grip on the rail, squatted, and stretched his free hand down to uncouple the rear car from the train.

He was naturally aboard the coach car still going somewhere as the club car began to fall back on the uphill grade. He resisted an impulse to wave bye-bye as the club car rolled to a halt, hesitated, then rolled back the other way. It might jump the tracks before it reached Tepic. Then again, it might not. Gaston moved innocently inside the car ahead to sit down and think about that.

In her private compartment, up forward, Pilar moaned, "Oh, that is too deep, *querido!* It has been so long since I have been with any man like this!"

Captain Gringo moved less passionately as he lay naked in her arms, with her slender ankles locked atop his rump. She said, "That's better. But I cannot believe I am letting a man I am not married to treat me like this in broad daylight! How did you get me out of my clothes so swiftly, Ricardo? I do not remember telling you I wished you to be so forward, even though you know I needed this!"

He didn't answer. High-class dames always talk like that at first. It would have been rude to point out that she'd started unbuttoning her bodice as soon as he'd kissed her. Or that she'd invited said kiss with the smoke signals in her dark Spanish eyes before he could get the damned door locked.

The mattress under her naked firm flesh was firm, too. So even though she had slim horsewoman's hips, her love gate was presented at a nice angle to his thrusts, and the click-clacking wheels under them vibrated her teasingly on his shaft even when he moved it gently in her. He wanted to make it last. She was the best he'd found since escaping from that gunboat, and she wouldn't be getting off for hours, thank God.

But the wheels were clicking slower now. The damned train seemed to be stopping at every village. He started moving in her at his own pace, on his own. She moaned, "Oh, that feels lovely. But why are we stopping, Ricardo?"

"We're not. I'm getting ready to *come*, baby!"

"Oh, me too! But if we stop at a station, someone might peek in!"

"The shades are down. Don't you remember pulling them down? Oh, yeah, I'm almost there!"

"Ay, Maria! Me too! I don't care if anyone's watching! I wish to come and, *madre mia*, I am coming!"

Out on the platform, Gaston was blissfully unaware of them as he ran over to the public pay phone and called police headquarters in Tepic. They said the runaway club car had indeed rolled into the Tepic yards and smashed into a box car, and they were mad as hell about it. When they asked who Gaston was, he said, "Lieutenant Verdugo, *Federale* Intelligence. There is no time to talk. I called you because there are no *federales* in Tepic. You must not let him get away!"

"Get away? Who is trying to get away, lieutenant?"

"The notorious Captain Gringo! I am about to leave the train to go after his confederate, another soldier of fortune. It is obvious what happened. As you can easily check with San Blas, a detachment of *Yanqui* navy police are aboard this train. When Captain Gringo saw them, he uncoupled the club car, hoping to coast back to town so he could catch a safer train. Ah, I see some *muchachos* with machetes, so I must organize a sweep of the hills for the other one! Be careful about the one who rode the club car back. He is armed, dangerous, and a most dreadful liar! Don't let him trick you!"

Then Gaston hung up and ran to catch the train as it started rolling. The conductor was standing on the rear platform. He said, "Hey, did you see what happened to the club car? It was there a minute ago!"

Gaston said, "I just called Tepic about it. They will arrest the *Yanqui* bastard who did it."

"You know who stole my club car, señor? Who on earth are you?"

"Keep it under your hat. I work for the government. But I promise you shall be shot if you breathe a word about it to anyone."

"Ah, in that case silence is golden, no? The other secret agent you came aboard with is up forward. Questioning a suspect, from the moaning sounds I just heard."

"*Bueno.* See they are not disturbed. We are on a mission of grave delicacy. If the woman talks, we may let her get off alive at her stop. But why am I telling you all this? Remember, not a word to anyone!"

So the conductor didn't go near Pilar's compartment again. He had his wife and kids to think of.

So, as Captain Gringo made undisturbed love up forward, Gaston kept a lookout in the forward coach, seated with his back to the bulkhead where he could watch for wandering U.S. sailors. None came. As he'd passed them a second time, they'd started a poker game. It would take them a while to miss their officer. Gaston doubted they'd miss him much.

Meanwhile, back in Tepic, the police, who had their own wives and kids to think of, had turned the case over to the tougher *rurales.* Lieutenant Carson laughed like hell when they told him he was Captain Gringo. He faced the trio of hard-faced men in big gray sombreros who'd just led him to the end of the tracks and said, "This is ridiculous! I am not Walker. I'm a U.S. Navy officer, you idiots!"

The *rurales* exchanged thoughtful glances. Carson took out his I.D. and said, "Here, if you can't read, maybe the pictures will help. You see that American eagle? Take me to your superior! You're fucking with the U.S. Navy, and nobody fucks with the U.S. Navy unless they like noise!"

One of the *rurales* smiled gently and said, "We have heard this. Yesterday, just up the coast, a *Yanqui* gunboat shelled a *rurale* post. Many of our comrades were killed, Señor U.S. Navy. Perhaps you would like to tell us why you shelled *rurales?* It seems a most cruel thing to do, in peacetime, no?"

Carson muttered, "Jesus!" then pasted a smile across his face and said, "Hey, guys, that wasn't my outfit! I don't know anything about any, ah, misunderstanding like that."

"It was nothing to be misunderstood, señor. The shells came down. The men inside went up, through the roof. We understand you *Yanquis* do not seem to like us. It is not important. We don't like you either."

One of the others muttered, "Enough. Why do we waste time with this gringo, eh?"

Carson pleaded, "No, wait! Please!" as the *rurale* drew his .45 and cocked it. Carson dropped to his knees, whimpering, "You're arresting the wrong man!"

The *rurale* looked puzzled as he growled, "Arrest? What is this arrest shit?" and pulled the trigger.

Carson's face vanished in gunsmoke. When the smoke cleared, he was stretched out at their feet, still twitching. The man who'd shot him spat and said, "Bueno. That is how one deals with big-mouth *Yanquis,* no?"

One of his comrades said, "We should have questioned him some more, first. Now we'll never know whether he was this Captain Gringo or some other gringo mother-fucker!"

The man who'd shot Carson holstered his gun, saying, "You must be new at this game, *niño*. We must wire Ciudad Mexico as soon as we find someone to bury this carrion. *El presidente* will be pleased to learn Captain Gringo is dead."

"But, Paco, he said he was someone else, and now, with his face blown off, it may be difficult to tell if he told the truth or not, no?"

"*Estupido!* That tip *said* he was a big liar. Of course he was Captain Gringo. A real *Yanqui*-gunboat man would have never identified himself as such to us after shelling one of our posts! This renegade could not have known about the international incident, so he outsmarted himself with some stolen I.D. They told us he escaped from a *Yanqui* gunboat, remember? Look at him. You can still see he was tall and blond in life. He fits the damned description. The case is closed. The renegade is dead. So nobody has to look for him anymore. But let us get out of this hot sun, *muchachos*. The shooting of gringos is thirsty work, even though it gives one pleasure."

5 EXCITING ADVENTURE SERIES
MEN OF ACTION BOOKS

__NINJA MASTER
by Wade Barker
Committed to avenging injustice. Brett Wallace uses the ancient Japa-
nese art of killing as he stalks the evildoers of the world in his mission.
__#4 MILLION-DOLLAR MASSACRE   (C30-177, $1.9
__#5 BLACK MAGICIAN   (C30-178, $1.9

__THE HOOK
by Brad Latham
Gentleman detective, boxing legend, man-about-town. The Hook cross
1930's America and Europe in pursuit of perpetrators of insurance frau
__#1 THE GILDED CANARY   (C90-882, $1.9
__#2 SIGHT UNSEEN   (C90-841, $1.9
__#5 CORPSES IN THE CELLAR   (C90-985, $1.9

__S-COM
by Steve White
High adventure with the most effective and notorious band of milit.
mercenaries the world has known—four men and one woman with a p
fect track record.
__#3 THE BATTLE IN BOTSWANA   (C30-134, $1.9
__#4 THE FIGHTING IRISH   (C30-141, $1.9
__#5 KING OF KINGSTON   (C30-133, $1.9
__#6 SIERRA DEATH DEALERS   (C30-142, $1.9

__BEN SLAYTON: T-MAN
by Buck Sanders
Based on actual experiences, America's most secret law-enforcem
agent—the troubleshooter of the Treasury Department—combats
enemies of national security.
__#1 A CLEAR AND PRESENT DANGER   (C30-020, $1.9
__#2 STAR OF EGYPT   (C30-017, $1.9
__#3 THE TRAIL OF THE TWISTED CROSS   (C30-131, $1.9
__#5 BAYOU BRIGADE   (C30-200, $1.9

__BOXER UNIT—OSS
by Ned Cort
The elite 4-man commando unit of the Office of Strategic Studies wh
dare-devil missions during World War II place them in the vanguard of
action.
__#3 OPERATION COUNTER-SCORCH   (C30-128, $1.
__#4 TARGET NORWAY   (C30-121, $1.

The Best of Adventure
by RAMSAY THORNE

DIRTY HARRY
by Dane Hartman

Never before published or seen on screen.

He's "Dirty Harry" Callahan—tough, unorthodox, no-nonsens
plain-clothesman extraordinaire of the San Francisco Poli
Department...Inspector #71 assigned to the bruising, thankle
homicide detail...A consummate crimebuster nothing can st
—not even the law!